D0642750

HE DIGS
A
HOLE

Danger Slater

FUNGASM
press

FUNGASM PRESS
an imprint of Eraserhead Press
PO Box 10065
Portland, OR 97296

www.fungasmpress.com
facebook/fungasmpress

ISBN: 978-1-62105-256-2
Copyright © 2018 by Danger Slater
Cover copyright © 2018 Katie McCann
Edited by John Skipp

Printed in the USA.

ACKNOWLEDGMENTS

Special thanks to John Skipp, for once again guiding me with his creative wisdom and editing talent, and helping to get this book into people's hands; and to my girlfriend Lisa LeStrange, who not only put up with me while in the process of writing this thing, but was the first person to read it and give me notes. Her input was invaluable.

85% of this book was written in the Midland branch of the Multnomah County Library in Portland, OR, so a big thank you to them for providing me with free wifi and air-conditioning while I slogged through my first, and second, and third drafts.

Thanks also to Rose O'Keefe, Katie McCann, Lori Hettler, Garrett Cook, Michael Allen Rose, Ophelia Darkly, Jon James, my family, and anyone else who has helped facilitate or bolster my artistic pursuits, in even the smallest capacity.

For Lisa

"We shall not cease from exploration,
And the end of all our exploring
Will be to arrive where we started
And know the place for the first time."

—T.S. Eliot, *Little Gidding*

PART ONE
ABOVE

1

The story goes like this:

Harrison Moss swallowed a seed. It didn't taste very good, but he swallowed it nonetheless. It traveled down his esophagus and into his stomach, where it germinated, inside of his body.

Then he started digging a hole in his backyard and he didn't know why.

It was not a very deep hole.

No, not at first.

But one day…one day…one day it certainly would be.

One day, this hole will be deep and wide and black and empty. One day, the edges of it will crumble apart like the crusts on an old birthday cake. One day, when this hungry earth can no longer suppress its own appetite and it's finally forced to devour itself, you'll look back at this moment – at the very first chapter of the book that you now hold in your hands – and know that here is where it all began.

This is the hole that will rebel against the sunshine.

This is the hole that will steal away the world in one apocalyptic gulp.

Look inside of it, if you dare!

Your gaze will fall into this hole and never come back out.

It was past midnight. In the summer. One of those sticky kind of nights where the air was as thick as swamp water and walking felt more akin to swimming.

Harrison Moss was asleep, but he was not dreaming. He had

stopped dreaming years ago. "What would be the point?" he might say, if you were to ask him why. He already knew what lay on the other side of that night's slumber. Tomorrow, and the next tomorrow, and every other tomorrow to come after that, all lined up in a perfectly predictable row.

The future was something he was certain would arrive.

Because life until that point had been nothing if not comfortable. He had a wife. He had a job. He had heat and electricity and thick walls to protect him. I'm not going to sit here and judge a person for coveting those things. As unremarkable as these suburbs were, at least they were normal. They were easy. They were safe.

Of course, one could also look at the world around Harrison, with its cookie-cutter houses and flawlessly manicured lawns, and find the whole thing suffocatingly dull. I certainly wouldn't judge a person for thinking that, either.

My point is, what ameliorated some might set others to stew, and what provided him relief might cause you distress. Happiness was often malleable like that, with no firm recipe from which it was fashioned. I'm not here to tell *you* exactly how to feel in this moment, I merely wish to inform you that for our protagonist, Harrison Moss, this meant that there was no place left in his head for dreams, and that his sleep was as vast and as dark as any hole could ever hope to be.

But on the night that he swallowed the seed, he suddenly found himself awake and anxious. Eyes wide and heart racing. His brain seemed to crackle with a dull kind of electricity, and yet his thoughts felt unfamiliar and distant, as if they existed in the fog of some bay, stranded unto islands all their own.

He swung his feet around and stood up. Tabitha didn't move. She didn't even stir. He probably could've dropped a cinderblock on her head and she wouldn't have even noticed, just let it slip from his fingers and then *SPLAT!* But where would he find a cinderblock at this hour?

Anyway, she was out cold, snoring gently, fast in the folds of their marital sheets.

He climbed out of bed. Moved purposefully, silently, as lithe and elusive as the shadows on the walls, a shadow himself. Not even a creak on the floorboards dared to give his position away. The wood beneath his feet remained stiff but loyal as he crept through the hallway and down the stairs.

Outside, he went.

It was as hot in the backyard as it was in the house. A delicate breeze tussled what was left of his thin, greasy hair. His pale skin looked even paler under the unguarded light of the moon. He looked anemic, like he was made of smoke and ash. He looked like he was already a ghost.

He stood there for a moment in just his underwear, papery and silver, and let the night heat paint his body in sweat. And he could hear them. Voices. Muffled. Coming from underneath the dirt.

The words they said were not spoken aloud. If you were standing next to him, you wouldn't have heard a thing.

Rather, for Harrison Moss, it sounded like a thousand separate voices had arrived in an instant. Like a subway car had just let out inside of his head. It didn't strike him as odd then, though on any other night it certainly would have. Such is life, in the first chapter of this book. Such is life, after swallowing the seed.

Every single one of these voices was saying the exact same thing. *To the shed. Go to the shed.*

It wasn't a conversation. It was a command.

Now in the shed:

Hedge clippers and weed whackers and great swooping loops of green rubber hose hanging down from the ceiling like cheap Christmas garland. A sepia-tinted mist demarcated the thin line between the shed's 40-watt glow and the encroaching darkness of the evening beyond.

Harrison Moss pulled a small gardening trowel from his toolbox and inspected it. The metal had begun to oxidize around the edges. No one had touched it in years, if they ever had ever touched it in the first place. Sometimes he bought things and never used them. This shed was full of tools that were never used, and yet, time set to rust them anyway. Everything that existed in this universe existed inside of entropy's rotten jaws.

As if to emphasize this, Harrison Moss picked up the trowel and held it up to the light. A few corroded screws were the only thing left connecting the head of it to its splintering handle.

He then inspected his own arms. Once powerful and strong, they now too seemed so fragile and useless. Decaying shafts of skin and bone stretched from his tried hands to his sloping shoulders. Time had begun to rust him away, too.

The seed in his stomach twisted and turned. It made him feel ill, but not ill enough to get sick. The voices under the dirt kept whispering.

Don't be afraid. No need for fear. No pain. No fear.

He looked to his right. There sat a single switch on the wall. He flicked it upward and a previously powerless chop saw in the corner of the room suddenly sprung to life.

WHIRRRRRRRRR!

Like a swarm of invisible insects, the deafening buzz of the rotating power tool filled up the shed.

The blade of the chop saw was a blur of blue and gray as it spun around and around.

He set his eyes to the machine. Tried to follow its ever-quickening movement, an impossible task at its current speed. He stared until his vision spun too, rendering him momentarily too dizzy to move. Still, he watched the blade, as if he were hypnotized.

Harrison Moss was suddenly overcome with an immense sense of clarity. Of calm. He couldn't explain it, not just because he didn't fully understand it, but also because he hadn't the vocabulary. Still, he could most assuredly feel it; that much could not be denied. He didn't need a dictionary to know there was poetry in this moment. Something tantric. Something cosmic. An indefinable feeling in which everything seemed to click into place, almost as if they sky above and the ground below had somehow learned to sing in unison…

…or maybe that wasn't exactly right. Maybe the sky and the ground were always in harmony, and he had only figured out how to listen…

Harrison Moss was going to be okay. He had never felt more certain. And then he shoved both of his hands into the whirling blade.

Oatmeal-thick clumps of wet, warm flesh splattered against the walls like they had been tossed by a defiant child.

Blood surged from his wrists in crimson spates, soaking into the ground, covering his bare chest, staining his face red so that just the whites of his eyes shone like lighthouses through the clotting gore. The smell of copper surfaced up from the mineshafts in his body. Cold steel chewed through his hands and vomited them back out, and still he dug in deeper. He pushed forward harder. He didn't even wince as the blade ripped through his palms and sent his fingers pointing in opposite directions before severing them completely and shooting them off into the darkness.

And then, once he was finally and irreparably maimed, once he had no hands left at all, he pulled away. The machine stopped shrieking. The chop saw came to a halt. For the moment, all that existed was the sound of his breath and his rapidly beating heart.

Bracing the tool against the wall, he thrust the wooden handle of the gardening trowel into the end of his open left wrist. Loose skin hung around it like the sleeve of a tunic. Displaced meat bubbled out like jelly around the trowel's base. Harrison buried the tool into the mutilated stump, pushing in as far as it would go, until it nestled itself tightly between his radius and his ulna. It felt almost as if his bones were reaching for it. Like they were trying to grab it and hold on. Like his skeleton was a separate entity from him and his body was merely the terrarium in which it grew.

Then he did the same thing to his right hand, this time inserting a cultivator, a tiny stainless-steel garden rake, its three-forked prongs stretching out like a crooked claw.

Out in the backyard again. Out into the night.

He stood there, in the center of his lawn. Air filled his lungs. In and out. The grass danced around his toes. Moist. Writhing. He bent down and got in close. So close he was almost hugging it. And he saw that it was not grass that surrounded his feet at all. The entire ground was covered with worms. Hundreds of them. Thousands even, squirming over each other like a living tapestry. His whole yard was moving.

He brushed them to the side, slime coating his already blood-damp skin, to reveal the cold dirt underneath. Harrison Moss slowly slipped the spaded end of his new shovel hand into the soil. It passed into the earth as easily as a knife passing into butter.

"It really is a lovely evening, isn't it?" he said to the worms.

And he dug.

2

There is one other thing that warrants a mention, before we continue on to the next chapter, and beyond.

On the night that Harrison began digging his hole, he saw someone watching him, from the darkness. It was a lady. But it was not his wife. This lady was…something else.

Yes, that's a better descriptor. She was some*thing* else, not some*one* else. Because although the energy that surrounded her was decidedly feminine, she always remained far enough away that any of her distinguishing features were obscured by shadows. Harrison couldn't even tell if she was human in shape, though if she wasn't human, what shape could she be?

She was in the bedroom with him when he first woke up, floating off to the side of his bed, where the sliver of moonlight from the window couldn't reach.

She was in the shed with him. He could feel her presence, even though then he couldn't see her at all. It was as if she was made of pure vibrations, as if she only existed in the screeching of the chop saw as it bounced off the claustrophobic wood walls.

And she was certainly there in the backyard as Harrison's newly repurposed hands burrowed and gouged their way into the Earth. She watched him, silently. She lingered, faintly.

Of course, with all the thoughts charging through his head at the time, Harrison hardly even noticed her. She was no more intrusive than the fog is loud.

He stayed fastidious in his task. Feverish, even. Determined to dig.

And as sure as the world kept turning, dig he did.

3

It was several hours later when the morning reached its gilded fingers around the horizon and cracked it open like the shell of an egg. Daylight spilled across the sky. The paperboy delivered the paper. A chorale of robins sang.

The earthworms that filled his yard the night before had long since retreated back to wherever it was they had come from. As did the phantasmagorical "woman" who watched him. She had evaporated, alongside the morning dew…

…okay, okay, okay, she didn't *actually* evaporate alongside the morning dew. That was me employing poetic license, turning a phrase, creating a slightly more colorful variation of the *exact* facts in order to elicit from you a fuller emotional response.

Was it successful?

The point is, she was gone, and there was no trace left of her at all.

"Harry?" Tabitha said, her voice cutting like a katana through the hemorrhaging dawn.

Harrison kept digging, completely oblivious to the fact that his bewildered wife had been watching him for the past five minutes.

"Harrison?" she said again, louder.

Still digging, he was undaunted. Scoop by scoop by scoop by scoop.

"HARRISON MOSS, ARE YOU LISTENING TO ME!?"

Harrison stopped and looked up towards her, squinting against the glare of the rising sun.

Tabitha stood on the deck in just her bathrobe. Mug of steaming black coffee in hand. Head tilted slightly to the side, seemingly offset by the weight of her crooked and accusatory eyebrows. She didn't look happy, that much was clear.

"Why are you yelling at me?" Harrison said. "I'm standing right here."

"What the hell are you doing?"

He rubbed the sweat from his forehead and motioned to the meter-deep ditch he had dug out overnight.

"I'm digging a hole," he replied.

"Yeah, I can see that," said Tabitha. "But why?"

"Huh?"

"Why are you digging a hole?"

He paused, then said, "Well, jeez, I don't know, Tabs."

"You don't know?" she asked. "What do you mean, you don't know?"

"Why does anyone do anything?"

"What?"

"Look, I woke up last night and I had this…*feeling*. Inside my head. Inside my body. And it made me want to dig a hole. So I did. You ever get like that? You ever get a *feeling*, Tabitha?"

"Have I ever gotten a *feeling*?"

"How can I explain it?" he said. "It was like there was this THING that was buzzing around in my head. Like a mosquito or a gnat or somethin'. But it was less defined than a mosquito. It didn't have a body or anything like that. Instead, it was lighter than air and made up of all shadows. An' when I tried to look at it straight on, it slipped right through the cones in my eyes like it were a color that shouldn't exist."

"What are you talking about?"

He continued, unabated.

"This THING, this INVISIBLE THING, you know it's there, but you don't quite understand it. It don't make no sense to you. And so you write it off. You ignore it like you ignore the million other things that float through your head an' just go about your day like it's any other day. And that might work for a minute. Might even work for years, if you're lucky. You walk around and smile and everything seems fine, and shit, maybe everything *is* fine because that's what we've built here together, Tabitha, a fine life – but suddenly, there this thing is again. A dark wave. A *tidal* wave. And that's when you realize that this thing you've been tryin' so hard for so long to ignore is actually filling you up. Filling up your whole body. An' now it's everywhere. It's in your lungs as you breathe and on your lips when you speak and it's running through your veins like it's got on track shoes, and not only can you NOT avoid it anymore, but you ARE it. You are IT, Tabitha. You are THE THING. An' it ain't even a choice after that. You have to do what it tells you, even if it's not directly tellin' you to do anything. Do you understand what I'm tryin'ta say to you?"

She looked from her dirt-covered husband to the hole in the center of her now ripped-up lawn.

"You're making a mess out here," she said.

"Well of course I'm making a mess," he replied. "I'm not done yet."

4

In the corner of the Moss' backyard there grew a peculiar-looking tree that bore from its branches a peculiar-looking fruit.

This fruit was as purple and meaty as a human spleen. Dozens of these fruits dangled above, doing their best to imitate the stars as they pulsated and throbbed.

The tree from which they hung was a big tree. Thicker and taller, by far, than any other tree in the neighborhood. Its bark looked like skin. Like a tan layer of goose-freckled flesh that had been stretched and wrapped around a monolith of sturdy, but errant, bone. It felt like skin too.

This strange tree was pliable in ways trees usually weren't. Were you to strike it, a welt would form. In the summertime, greasy droplets of liquid would condense along its shaft, as if it were sweating. And perhaps most disturbing of all, were the branches that sprouted from its highest boughs, which appeared to be made up of human fingers. Long, crooked fingers, growing out of one another like river distributaries. The longer ones had over 20 knuckles running up and down their digits, bent in impossibly twisted directions. When the breeze would blow, the branches would thrum against the trunk. During a hurricane, it sounded like a round of applause.

The tree was there when the Mosses moved in.

They didn't plant it. They didn't even know what type of tree it was.

Harrison went to the library once, to do some research on it. See if he could figure out its name, identify its origin, learn something—*anything*—

about it at all. He spent the afternoon nose-deep in an encyclopedia, scouring the internet, rifling through books on biology and botany, flipping past page after page in the most arcane texts available on the subject of floral-arboreal nomenclature. All of this, of course, to no avail. This tree was a one-of-a-kind type of timber, unclassifiable by any known resource, growing exclusively in their backyard. As far as Harrison Moss could tell, taxonomically speaking, it didn't even exist.

All the other houses in the cul-de-sac in which they lived had sycamores that lined their property. Stout and verdant, covered in bushy branches so thick that the leaves were forced to cascade over one another like a great, green waterfall.

These plants were so plentiful, and so perfectly and purposefully placed, that this street couldn't have had any other name except Sycamore Lane. So that's what the people who designed the neighborhood had decided to call it. Shaded and quiet. Predictable and secure. Could there be anywhere in the world more inviting, or more benign, than a street named Sycamore Lane?

But the House of Moss sat like a pimple on the pastel face of this seemingly idyllic suburb.

It wasn't the fault of its current residents, who until the moment Harrison swallowed the spleenfruit seed from this bizarre tree and started digging his mysterious hole, were just as boring as the rest of their neighbors. Nor was it the fault of the building itself; the two-story colonial with the cadaver-colored shingles that hung from its front like tags of skin. The house was as homogenized and antiseptic as the ones that lay to the left and the right of it. Totally normal.

No, it was that tree – that big ugly monster tree with its strange and fleshy fruit – that set this property apart from the rest.

Tabitha had asked the realtor about it as she and Harrison had first toured the house. They had already been through the kitchen and living room, the cellar and foyer, up the stairwell, down the hall, in and out of every bedroom and every bath, then past the threshold of the backdoor. Into the backyard.

"The tree was here when the neighborhood was built," the realtor told them. "We've had surveyors out here more than once. We're still not 100% sure on the full extent of its breadth, or how deep down it goes. It's a big ol' bastard, that's for sure. In fact, there's a good chance the root structure stretches from yard to yard like an underground parking garage. It could secretly be growing underneath every house in the cul-de-sac. The other residents wouldn't even know it."

"But is it safe?" asked Tabitha.

"Safe?" the relator laughed. "Darling, I wouldn't be surprised if this tree was the only thing keeping the land here from collapsing in on itself."

"Oh."

The relator then leaned in conspiratorially. "Plus—and you won't see this on any of the official paperwork—but, when we first tried to cut it down, the most unusual thing happened…"

"What?" asked Tabitha, eyes wide.

"It started to bleed," the realtor replied with a raised eyebrow before quickly changing the subject back to the building. "Anyway, as you can see, the oversized two-car garage is perfect for housing any vehicle you could possibly desire, from a Mini Cooper to a Humvee…"

Years later, Tabitha still thought the tree was creepy.

The way it cast shadows across her kitchen. The gnarled finger-branches reaching out from the top. It looked as if it were trying to pluck the sun right out of the sky. There was something foreboding about it. Something sinister. Malicious, even. And those disgusting fruits…she refused to touch them. They'd sometimes ripen and fall from the tree's upmost branches, landing with such force it was almost as if they had been thrown. They'd splatter against the ground. Rupture open. White seeds the size of marbles would spill out. Fleshy pearls encased by quivering pulp. She had seen Harrison shifting through a pile once. He was outside, on his knees, like a dog. Face almost buried in the rotten paste. He pulled up a seed and inspected it closely, like it were a rare gem he just found. Tabitha couldn't understand how he could hold it so close to his nose without getting sick. To her, the spleenfruit smelled worse than anything she had ever smelled before.

To her, the spleenfruit smelled like death.

5

Harrison Moss sat at the kitchen table, face and torso caked in mud.

Tabitha took the seat across from him, but didn't say anything. His breath seemed to hiss like hydraulic brakes as it was forced through the twisted passageways of his nose. Aside from that, there was silence.

A few triangular pieces of toast sat on a plate between them. Harrison raised an eyebrow. Tabitha motioned for him to eat it. He reached out and snatched them up. Shoved all of them into his mouth at the same time. Breathing even louder, struggling to chew, smacking his lips together like a fish dragged to land. His wife looked away, disgusted.

"Jesus, Harrison…"

"I'm hungry, Tabitha," he said. "I've been working all night."

"Working?"

"This hole certainly ain't gonna dig itself."

Tabitha took a sip of her coffee and ground her teeth together as she listened to him wheezing through the food stuffed into his cheeks.

"Can I ask you a question?" she finally said.

Harrison's chewing slowed, then stopped. He forced the half-masticated wad down his throat.

"What?" he said.

"Did you chop off your hands and replace them with a gardening tools?"

"Did I—"

He held up his hands. One a shovel. One a rake. A tiny piece of buttered toast still impaled on the end of one of his cultivator's prongs.

"Yeah. I suppose I did."

"Don't you think you should've maybe…ya know…discussed it with me before you went ahead and made such an extreme and irreversible body modification?"

"Maybe," he shrugged. "Hey, do we have any eggs to go with this?"

"Maybe?" she said. "What do you mean *maybe*?"

"First off, it's not all *THAT* extreme of a modification," he replied. "It's just my hands. It's not like—I dunno—I pulled out my appendix or gallbladder or anything like that. Secondly, I didn't know I needed to ask your permission every time I want to dig a hole or remove one of my appendages. I'm not a child, Tabitha, and I am perfectly capable of taking care of myself without you policing my every move. Although, truth be told, I've been thinking about replacing my legs too. Maybe putting drilling augers there, right under my knees. Ya know, so I could dig even faster…"

"Do not cut off your legs!"

"Ugh. You see? This is *exactly* what I'm talking about."

They lapsed back into silence. Staring at each other. Harrison took a loud sip of coffee.

"So where are they?" she asked.

"Where are what? The hole?"

"Your hands, Harrison. Where are your hands?"

"Still on the floor of the shed, I'd reckon," he said. "Chopped up into a dozen little pieces and splattered against the wall."

"Oh Jesus…"

"There ain't no reconciling this, Tabs," he said. "What's done is done. It was actually pretty brutal, now that I think about it. The damn things didn't want to come off. I had to really shove 'em in there deep. I suspect even *you'd* be able to find some sorta comfort in that, since you're obviously the kind of person who wants her hands to stay attached to her body."

Tabitha shook her head in disbelief and pointed to the space where his left hand once was.

"You know, that was the hand your wedding ring was on."

Harrison looked at the shovel, turned back to her.

"So it was."

"Well I'm just going to come right out and say it: I don't understand this behavior, Harry. This sudden fervor. This impulsivity. This isn't like you."

"Sudden? You think this is sudden?" he smiled, dirt in the cracks between his teeth. "There ain't nothin' sudden happening here at all. What looks like impulsivity to you is nothing but the inevitable end of a long and uncomfortable dream. I tossed and turned my way to this point, even if you couldn't tell because I looked like I was asleep. I'm ain't here by mistake, Tabitha. I haven't succumbed to an illness or an accident. This ain't no psychotic break. I woke up and looked outside. It's morning."

"What the hell are you even talking about? Are you Mr. Philosophy now? Speaking to me in riddles? Acting all cryptic, like I'm supposed to be seduced or intrigued by any of this nonsense? You think you're Jean-Paul Sartre all of a sudden? Or fucking Plato?" She shook her head and exhaled dramatically. "Telling me you 'had to wake up,' as if espousing some bullshit phrase like that means a goddamn thing in the real world?"

He shrugged, unfazed.

"Harry, you didn't even get dressed this morning. And you're certainly not at the office like you're supposed to be. Today is no different than every other day that came before it. You know this. And I know you, Harrison. I know the REAL you. This isn't right. This isn't normal…"

Before she could finish her sentence, Harrison's spine stiffened suddenly, as if loaded on a spring, and he pressed the backside of his rake hand to his wife's lips. The cold steel against her skin shushed her almost immediately. His paranoid eyes quickly darted back and forth. His chest heaved in and out, faster. His nostrils flared.

"Wha–" she started to say.

"Tabitha," he said as his gaze fell back on her. "Tell me you can hear them."

"Hear who?"

"Them. The voices."

"What voices?" she shouted.

"The voices in the backyard. Coming up from under the ground. They're inside my head. They're ones who've been talking to me all night. The ones who told me to dig."

"That does it," Tabitha stood up and grabbed the telephone off the receiver. "I'm calling Dr. Caterwaul. You're sick in the brain, Harrison Moss. You need professional help."

In a single fluid motion, Harrison spun out of his chair and slammed his shovel hand into the wall, severing the phone line. Tabitha looked at him, her round face full of fear, mouth slightly open in shock as the curly cut wire dangled between them.

"Harrison, you're scaring me…"

"They're screaming," he said, his voice barely above a whisper. "They're screaming for me, right now."

"Wha – what are they saying?" she whispered back.

He closed his eyes and concentrated, as if somehow, in the fresh darkness, the voices could be heard more clearly. When he opened them again to look at his wife, a muddy tear rolled down his cheek before falling off the end of his chin.

"They want me to join them," he said, then added "They want *us* to join them."

6

Let's work backwards.

Let's take a look at Tabitha Moss earlier that morning, as she woke to find her husband's side of the bed empty. The bottom sheet flat and unwrinkled. As if he had never been there at all.

Let's watch silently as Tabitha sat up and sniffed the air. She couldn't smell him, the cumulative stress of the day before fermenting in his pores overnight, filling the room. She sniffed again. Nothing. He was gone. He'd been gone for hours.

This entire scene played out very early, before the dawn had crested over the distant city skyline. Before she knew he was in the backyard, digging.

She listened closely. Only quietude. The house they shared was haunted by nothing. Not the apneic snuffling of her slumbering groom. Not the creaks of his heavy feet as they plodded across the floor. Not the steady whisper of the shower's steam as it passed through the crack at the bottom of the closed bathroom door. She looked at the clock. He couldn't be at work yet. The bus downtown didn't leave for another hour and a half. And so she thought:

Maybe he had left her. Maybe he was gone for good.

He could've easily packed up a suitcase while she was still sleeping and slunk his way out the door without a peep. He could've chartered a taxi and told the man behind the wheel to just keep driving, and down the highway they would've roared, until the two of them plummeted off the edge of the world. He could've hitchhiked his way to the middle of a desert so he could live on his belly among the scorpions and snakes. He could be in jail. He could be dead.

She let that particular thought echo in her head for a while. He could be dead. DEAD. D-E-A-D. Her husband, the corpse. Her husband, the water-logged body at the bottom of a lake. Her husband, the lunch buffet for a flock of hungry buzzards. He was gone, that much was certain, and she had no idea where he was. For all she knew, she may never hear from him again. She imagined what that would be like: her life, from this moment on, without him there, feeding on her emotional wellbeing like a parasite chewing through her heart. And although she didn't leap up from the sheets to express this notion out loud – although she barely allowed herself to acknowledge such a vile and destructive notion internally – the thought of his face, his stupid sullen face now rendered bloated and blue and cold and dead, made her smile.

But let's go back even farther than that.

Let's talk about last year. And the year before that. And all the years that led up to the day when Harrison Moss swallowed a spleenfruit seed and started digging a hole in his backyard. Because Harrison Moss had not always been the type of man who sought to dismantle the Earth. Before he began this absurd and all-consuming endeavor, he had lived a life that, by all comparative definitions, would've been considered excessively *normal.*

Painfully, mind-numbingly, acquiescently normal.

Harrison would rise when the alarm let out its obnoxious bleat. He'd bathe. Shave. Squeeze his tired body into a business suit. His coffee was so black and hot that it would burn his throat like battery acid as he sucked it down.

Before he left he'd always kiss his wife on the top of her head. A sterile kiss. Perfunctory and passionless, like he was a wife-kissing-robot, programmed to dole out husbandly affection, one tiny fraction at a time. And she'd sit in her bathrobe and let his dry lips scratch against her scalp like there was still some comfort to be found in that. And as he walked out the door she'd offer him some exhausted valediction like "Have a good day at work, honey" and he'd say "I love you" and she'd say "I love you too" and the words would feel like cotton filling up their mouths.

And then we'd follow Harrison down the walkway to the local bus stop, where the other husbands in the neighborhood would already be standing, waiting to get picked up and taken to the office downtown.

"Mornin' Brad," Harrison would always say when he saw his neighbor, Brad Flatly.

"Mornin' Harry," Brad Flatly would always say back.

And the bus would *putter-putter* into the cul-de-sac and pull up to the curb and the door would open with a rusty screech and Harrison and Brad and the rest of the men of Sycamore Lane would line up in a single-file and they would board and the bus would drive off and soon the residential neighborhood would disappear, giving way to the gray towers of the abutting city, sticking up from the ground like vampire fangs. And they all went to work in the office, Monday through Friday, week after week.

This is the life that he had been working so hard to maintain. Year after year, decade by decade. This was the prize. The pot of gold at the end of the rainbow. The *and-they-lived-happily-ever-after* he had always been promised at the end of every fairy tale he ever read.

Look, you get it.

You're not stupid; I KNOW you get it.

You're a savvy reader, and what I'm talking about here is well-worn territory in pretty much every facet of modern fiction. You have your main character – in this case, Harrison Moss: traditionally white, traditionally middle-class, traditionally male – encumbered by some tedious and ill-defined version of "existential ennui," which leads him, unsurprisingly, to certain personal revelations, a "peeling back of the curtains" so that the "dark underbelly" of the suburbs can be finally exposed:

OooOOOooo, so edgy!

We've all been here before, literature-wise. Probably by the time you graduated from 10th grade, if not sooner. So, if you're looking for a long digression that thoroughly explores this thesis, please go read *Death of a Salesman* or watch *American Beauty* or consume one of the SEVERAL THOUSANDS of other books and movies that deal with this particular topic. Arthur Miller did it way better than I'm ever going to, and he did it a half century before I did. So although this office, this job, this commute, and this routine had already taken up large swaths of Harrison's life thus far, in the grander scheme of things that THIS PARTICULAR novel has left to say, it is all rather irrelevant.

So instead of that boring old trope, let's talk about the day that Harrison and Tabitha's genitalia disappeared.

Or maybe disappeared is the wrong word. It was more like they…*healed over.*

This happened years ago. Before the morning that Tabitha woke up alone. Before Harrison cut off his hands and replaced them with a gardening tools. Long before he began to dig.

It wasn't immediate. A magician didn't come by and wave his wand like *abracadabra* and then *poof* both of their bits were suddenly flat-patched. There was no horror in this discovery either. No shrieking morning, after the Sex Organ Bandit absconded away in the night. It was more like…a slow recession. The ebbing of a tide. A mountain eroding. The penis retreating back into the body, the vagina closing itself up like two tectonic plates that had been pushed together. Their genitals receding, until the only thing both of them contained between their legs was just smooth skin, raw and red, like mosquito bites. They hardly even noticed.

But this wasn't always the case, of course.

Once upon a time, Harrison and Tabitha Moss were newlyweds. And they were full of passion. They would make love the same way that the thunder rolled in, slow and deep. They would make the windows shake and the earth tremble. Afterwards they would watch TV together, lounging on opposite ends the same couch, toes touching beneath the fleece blanket they shared.

At one point, this house was new. Or, rather, new to them.

They had just moved in. Boxes full of their possessions filled the garage. The neighborhood still felt alien, a welcoming yet strange landscape that these two lovers had suddenly landed in. Even the neighbors – what was their name? The Flatlys? – seemed incongruously, even farcically, friendly. They had greeted them with a basket full of muffins and big stupid mannequin smiles, mere minutes after the moving truck had arrived.

"Welcome to the neighborhood, buddy!" said Brad, forcing Harrison into a brotherly hug.

"OH MY GOD I LOVE YOUR DRESS!" his wife, Jennifer, screamed in Tabitha's face.

"How 'bout them Giants, huh?" Brad thrust a beer into Harrison's hand. "9-0 already this year. You think they'll take the conference?"

"Here's a helpful tip: grind up a fresh lemon in your garbage disposal to keep the smells of rotten food at bay," Jennifer said.

It was all so overwhelmingly pedestrian – these Space Invaders from Planet Normal – with their banal enthusiasm bubbling up all over their hapless new neighbors.

"That's not us, is it?" Harrison asked Tabitha later that night.

"Of course not," she laughed. "That'll never be us."

But within that very same week Tabitha found herself spinning circles in the center of the spare bedroom across the hall, scornfully inspecting the empty walls. Her eyebrows furrowed. Her lips in a pout.

The room was white. Too white. And she didn't like it.

"You need to relax, Tabs," Harrison said to her, leaning up against the doorframe. "Why do anything at all? The room looks just fine to me. Just like the other rooms. Everything is fine. White is a good color."

"White isn't a color," she said back to him.

"Not to get technical about it, but isn't white ALL of the colors, mixed-up in equal parts?"

"It doesn't work," she said. "It feels…unfinished…"

"Unfinished?"

"I just want to make this place ours, ya know?" She faced to her husband. "Cover up all the old shit that other people left here. Erase it. Start over fresh."

So she painted the room red. The color of passion.

But it didn't look right either. It still felt off; somehow wrong. Maybe it was because of the shadow spilling in through the window. Tabitha walked up and looked out. That nasty spleenfruit tree cast its shade directly into the room. Creeping across the floor and splashed out along the walls. It made it hard for her to see the colors in their truest hues. It was frustrating.

So she tinkered.

The red paint soon begat orange which soon begat yellow which soon begat green. Of course, that then begat the blue that begat the indigo which lead to the purple, and then back around again to the red, the shades subtly different tints every single time she passed through the rainbow, almost imperceptible, except to her: Crimson. Amber. Chartreuse. Cobalt. Lavender.

  Nothing felt right.

  She kept repainting it. Again and again.

Of course, if we're really going to go back, if we're *really* going to cast our sociological gaze on the point in which this relationship was forever and irreversibly doomed, we're going to have to go ALL the way back to the point BEFORE it was forever and irreversibly doomed. The point at which two broken people met each other for the very first time and decide that maybe they would feel less broken, together. This point is bigger in scope than just the stormy marriage of Harrison and Tabitha Moss, and although the moment you're about to read is quite specific to the two of them, this is actually the origin of all love. Because, no matter what we do, every tragedy started out as a comedy. And every pile of trash was once someone's treasure.

  So here we are on the day they met:

  We are in one of those big-box hardware stores. The kind with the sprawling black parking lots that take up huge tracts of real estate on the edge of town. Just one in a series of adjacent strip malls. Wal-Mart. Best Buy. Bed, Bath, and Beyond. These stores circled the suburbs like castle walls. Keeping people out. Or, maybe, keeping people in.

  We are in the Home Depot.

  We are in aisle 11.

  We are the invisible man floating behind Harrison Moss as he stood there in front of a massive rack, full of rope.

Young Harrison still had all his hair. Thick and brown, grown out and pushed back in a socially-acceptable state of distress. Sideburns squared up his jaw like that of an action figure. His body was svelte and clean. There were no wrinkles pinching the corners of his eyes. No gut to hang over the end of his belt. His confidence had not yet been eroded by the chisel-happy hand of time.

  He was there to buy tools. Perhaps a shovel. Perhaps a gardening trowel. He might need a gardening trowel one day. He didn't own one. He didn't even own a garden. But you never know.

Instead he ended up by the ropes. Staring at them.

And then there was Tabitha, stepping up next to him.

Young Tabitha –what a stunner!– her lips the color of grapefruit, parted slightly, revealing the peak of that crooked left incisor. Curvy and sensual. Soft, yet fearless. Her heterochromatic eyes, one green and one brown, eating and digesting the chain store's uninspired neon light differently. She was just distinctive enough to be her own beautiful breed.

Neither of them yet realized that this was one of those felicitous moments that blow in on sudden and nebulous winds; the kind that are able to permanently readjust the topography of the map of the world they had internally constructed. Neither one knew then that by the time this book has concluded that together they will have literally torn this world apart.

"It's almost like being in a cave, isn't it?" Harrison quietly said.

"Huh?" Tabitha replied, shooting a cautious glance towards the strange yet attractive man next to her.

"This store," he turned. "It's so big. An' these ropes are hanging down all over the place. Kinda look like vines, don't they? It's almost like we're in a cave. Like we're underground. There ain't a window around here. I doubt the sun has ever seen the spot we're standing in."

"I suppose," she shrugged. "Guess I never really thought about it before."

"Yeah, well, most people don't think about what's underground until they find themselves trapped in a pine box beneath it, an' that's just how it goes."

"So what are you, a geologist or something?"

"Ha ha. Nope," he said.

"Well why don't you enlighten me then…"

"Harrison."

"Enlighten me, Harrison, what do you know about the Earth that I don't?"

"Well, for one thing, it's everywhere."

"C'mon now, I know THAT much!" she giggled.

"Yeah, but have you ever *really* thought about it?"

"Of course. I'm thinking about it right now..." she replied.

"No, no, no, don't be silly. Look..." he said as he picked up a nearby plunger. He reached for her hand and she pulled back. He didn't flinch though, and he kept his open palm extended, looking at her with gentle eyes. After a moment, she let him take her tiny hand into his. He held her by the pointer finger and ran it in a circular motion around the rubber rim along the bottom edge. "See how the ground covers the entire Earth. And then there's us," he stopped her finger. "There's the tiny plot of land that we're on, right now. And we are so small, me and you. We only get to touch the surface of it."

She moved her finger away from his, dropping it down into the empty cavity in the center of the plunger head so that it hovered there, right in the middle.

"What about in here?" she said. "The world continues on inwardly for thousands of miles. And there's so much space in there. So many unknowns. So much left to explore. There is still so much mystery."

"Exactly," said Harrison. "And where there is mystery, there is hope. Anything is still possible beneath our feet."

"Anything?"

"Indeed."

"So you think there are caves shaped like Home Depots' inside the Earth?" she said.

He shook his head. "Could be. I don't know."

He put the plunger down. The two of them fell silent and their smiles slowly faded. Tabitha pulled a length of half-inch thick twine out of its spool and inspected as carefully as she would a parachute cord.

"It really is such a peculiar concept..." she said.

"What is?" Harrison asked.

"Death," she replied.

"Is it?"

"Think about it. We have the potential to do so much. It's right there in front of us. All these options. All these chances. And yet, most of us squander it away. We're afraid. Or distracted. Or we just lack the motivation to even try. And even if we have the desire, it somehow still seems...impossible. Being alive almost feels impossible. I wake up every day so goddamn confused as to how I even woke up at all."

"I don't happen to find death all that peculiar," Harrison said.

"No?"

"It's a simple equation with a zero sum. And it's universal; it reaches out and takes everyone with the same cold and calculated hand. If you're open to it, you'd be able to find beauty and symmetry in that."

"You find symmetry in the fact that, one day, you're going to die?"

"No. But I find symmetry in the sameness that death brings."

"But doesn't that seem unfair?" she said. "Doesn't the knowledge of your own mortality fill you up with an overwhelming sense of dread? Doesn't it consume you like it consumes me? How can we find meaning, find love, in the face of such hopelessness?"

"In the end," he said, pointing at the ropes. "We either let the fear destroy us or we do our best to distract ourselves from it. Because no matter how many lights we leave on at night, the darkness is still out there, waiting."

She bit the inside of her cheek and looked Young Harrison in his sad, hazel eyes.

"Look, I know I don't really know you," she said "But I was thinking, maybe we don't have to buy these ropes. At least, not today. We could…I dunno, maybe go out for a coffee together instead? And just talk?"

The ropes still hung

"We're only delaying the inevitable," he said.

"I know," she replied.

And they went and got coffee.

7

There was music hidden in every single scoop that Harrison pulled out of the ground.

If you were listening carefully, you could hear it too.

There was the staccato *swish* of his steel spade as it sliced into the dirt. The snare pop of his bones as he twisted his wrist. The mucousy sigh of the shifting terrain, almost as if the Earth itself were catching its breath between arias. It was a clandestine symphony, just beneath the soil.

Of course, all of that beauty was lost on Harrison Moss, who couldn't be bothered to listen at all. The man who was forcing the world to sing in his wake could only grunt and suffer as he worked. He was compelled to dig – he *needed* to dig – and he had been singularly focused on this task for the past week.

It had been four days since Harrison woke in the middle of the night and replaced his hands with a shovel and a rake. And it had been one day longer than that since he swallowed the mysterious seed from the spleenfruit tree.

And while the hole in his yard steadily grew larger by the minute, an entirely different narrative had been unfolding in concurrent time within the corridors of Harrison's own body:

At first it wasn't serious. Just a tickle in his stomach. Like he drank too much orange juice. No cause for alarm. And as the night proceeded on, as routinely as the nights before it, Harrison hadn't thought much of that peculiar tree or how its spleenfruit fell – as the spleenfruits often did – from the top of its highest branch.

It landed in front of him with a splat. A comet of meat. The impact splitting the rind open along its seam. Pink fleshy pulp spilled out. The stench of death, released in a malodorous instant. White seeds like fatty tumors rolled across the beryl-kissed lawn, almost like eggs. Like eyes. Like a bag full of eyeballs. Like the tree was looking at him from two dozen different angles at once.

Harrison stared at those seeds, and those seeds stared back at him.

It was a moment of weakness. He could've just ignored it. But those seeds. Those damn seeds with their unblinking eyes. They were dissecting him with a rotten gaze. He had to know what they were looking at.

And so he bent down. Dropped to his knees, like he was about to pray, and plucked a singular seed out of the goop. Just a single seed. Just one.

"You know there's nothing to see here that hasn't already been seen a thousand times before," he said out loud. "I am not a character in your storybook, and this is not a tale that some author is telling. I am just a simple man, in a simple house, living a simple life. Why would I want for more?"

This might've been wishful thinking on Harrison's part, because as evidenced by you reading these words right now, this clearly *is* a story being told. And stories, as I'm sure you know, often unfold in very measured and contrived ways. And it should be established by now that he was clearly a man in want of more. So perhaps it is with the knowledge that the plot must move on that Harrison Moss felt compelled to tilt back his head, extend his jaw, and drop the spleenfruit seed into his open mouth.

It rolled down his throat like a shot of whiskey. Swallowed into the pit of his stomach.

And the night continued.

And Harrison continued with it.

He ran on the treadmill and he watched Jeopardy! on the TV and when the clock struck 9:30 both he and Tabitha climbed into their bed and went to sleep. And all the while, that seed in his belly had begun to sprout. The casing split; opened up inside of him. It hatched. Wispy roots poked around his intestines, until they found their way into his bloodstream. They wrapped themselves around his veins like ivy, and crisscrossed his vision like strands of loose hair growing on the backside of his corneas. The roots snaked their way through his muscles and wreathed around his feeble bones before finding purchase in the folds of his slumbering brain.

It wasn't painful. Not at this point, at least. The seed grew as naturally as he was breathing. If I didn't just outright tell you about it, you would've had no idea there was anything going on inside of him at all. Tabitha certainly didn't. And neither, for that matter, did Harrison himself. He had stopped thinking about the seed almost as soon as he finished swallowing it. In fact, he might've never thought about it again were it not for the tiny leaf that sprung from the dark alley of his ear canal on the afternoon of that following Thursday as he stood there in the hole he had dug, now the size of a cemetery plot.

He plucked the leaf out with his rake hand and inspected it. Waxy and green, like poison sumac. He barely had enough time to contemplate the what-and-why of it all, to draw the tenuous chronological lines between seed and plant, before the wind came by and snatched it away. Sent it aflutter. Disappeared it into the sky.

The spleenfruit tree slowly clapped.

8

Tabitha watched Harrison.

Watched him for days as the hole in the backyard grew from a minor ditch to a 6-foot-chasm, then wider and deeper still, like an impact crater from a meteorite, concave on the bottom, raised up stiff and hard around the rim. There was no wavering in his resolve, and no inherent reasoning behind his behavior, at least not as far as Tabitha could discern.

"You know you're not supposed to be hearing voices," she said to him one afternoon as he continued to shovel downward. "The world isn't a radio that you're able to tune in and out of. Those screams you heard, inside your head, they don't exist."

He didn't say anything, so she continued, "You know they have a name for people who hear things that aren't there, right? They call them schizophrenics."

"Schizophrenia? No, no, no," he chuckled, his smile shining through the dirt that coated his face. "That's not what's happening here."

"What is happening here then?"

"What are we supposed to do when words start to fail us? How can we even feel emotions that we don't have the vocabulary to express? These voices I'm hearing, they're not even voices. They don't speak to me anymore than my own voice does. They—they're more like an idea. Or a compulsion."

"They want you to dig?"

"There is no *they*, Tabitha. That's what I'm getting at. *They* is *me*. There is no schism between my thoughts and my actions, between them and I. If control is the issue, then I'm piloting the ship. If anything, I might be piloting the ship for the first time." He stopped digging and held up his shovel hand so she could see it. "This is what a sane man does when he's run out of explanations and run out of options."

She motioned to the giant dirt pit in front of her.

"This is your definition of sanity?" she said.

"Foundations are laid underground, Tabs," he said.

"Burial plots are underground too."

"Don't be so dramatic."

"You're the one being dramatic!" she shouted. "You're the one destroying our yard."

"It's just a yard."

"But it's *our* yard."

"Is it?"

He then repeated the same mantra he had been saying to her since the excavation began:

"You have to trust me," he said.

And he continued to work.

But of course, she didn't trust him. How could she trust him? None of this made any sense to her. And although you have the luxury of looking upon this situation with the detached curiosity of a lazy anthropologist, Tabitha Moss had no other choice but to watch her husband in the backyard like a prisoner would watch their executioner sharpening an axe. What was he trying to accomplish with all of this? What was his endgame?

In a way, she blamed herself. How could she not? She wondered what she could've done to circumnavigate this crisis. And, in almost the same breath, she wondered if she could've avoided it at all.

She wondered: Where do I fit into this story? Am I the catalyst here? The fuse? The powder keg packed with TNT? Am I the creator, or the destroyer? Am I the victim, or the victimizer?

"Or maybe it's something else entirely," she mused aloud. Harrison was outside, shoulder deep in the ditch. She was standing in the kitchen and no one else was there. Well, no one else that is, except for YOU, the reader. So I guess that means she's talking directly to YOU. And even though the two of you aren't sharing the same physical space, even though it's all but impossible for the two of you to EVER share the same physical space, you are still the only one around to listen to her. And so you listen:

"You see, there was no cataclysm. No hard line drawn into the sand. No, you won't find any OBVIOUS reason that our marriage fell apart. That would be too simple, too convenient. And this isn't about convenience. This book is about the sticky-and-complicated in-betweens, the way things fall apart, the emotional gorge they leave behind, and the near-impossibility of filling that all back in, and everything else that was bound to transpire after the fairy tale ends."

Do you consider yourself broken?

It's not your voice asking that question. You don't have a voice. You are passively watching this whole story unfold. The thing is, a voice didn't actually ask her that question at all. But Tabitha continued to answer it regardless:

"I'm not broken. I sometimes feel like the only person in the world who isn't broken. Imagine how strong I must be to even keep up this charade to begin with? I am a rock, solid and unflappable. Of course, loneliness is intrinsic, wouldn't you agree? We are but one person, in a population of many. Loneliness is built into everyone, like Original Sin. It's the very fabric this human condition is sewn from."

She looked out the window at Harrison. From this angle, with his body hunched over, he looked like an animal.

"This certainly isn't the man I married. And not just physically, either. His confidence has been replaced by zealotry, his charisma has healed over like the bark on a birch tree, and whatever sickness has currently seized his bones seems to have seized his brains as well."

And, after all these years together, do you still consider yourself the same as you've always been?

"We got older. We both got older, sure. Can't help that. It's just the weight of all that innate loneliness, time certainly doesn't lighten that load, does it? It warps you, slowly but surely. Oh man, look at the backs of my hands…"

She holds up her hands for you to inspect. Fleshy and dry. Not like gardening tools at all.

"Look at those veins. Blue and distended. They're different than they used to look, but the blood inside them is still the same blood, isn't it? Inside, I'm still the same person I've always been. I'M THE SANE ONE HERE, not like that psychopath in the backyard, mutilating his body on purpose, upending our lives trying to answer to some absurd whim. You think I want to deal with our shitty relationship? God, no! But what are our options? Letting the darkness win? Waiting for some kind of freak accident to come along and take care of this decision for me? Someone has to be the glue that holds this house together. What is life if not the pursuit of normalcy?"

She continued:

"And plus, I have the spare room I'm still working on. I got my own projects I need to complete. I know it's been years, but I've almost figured out the perfect color. I'm, like, *right there* with it. And once I paint that room, I can move on to the rest of the house, and once I paint this whole house, we can finally get settled and truly call this place home. I though Granny Smith green was going to be it, but then I realized the room should be more of a key lime. Of course, that didn't feel right and I had to move onto a light jade, which ended up being too light, so I covered it with fern…"

Truth was, the man in the backyard had become a stranger to her long before he started to dig. And she had become stranger, too, with each new coat of paint she slathered on top of the last.

Loneliness was a disease for which there was no cure.

Tabitha noticed that the arm with the shovel on the end had taken on a pallid and sickly hue. She figured it was sepsis. Blood poisoning. Right around the nub, where the handle had been forcibly shoved into his skin, green pockets of pus had formed. Putrid slime ran down his rancid wrist.

"Infected green slime," Tabitha said. "Perhaps that's the color the spare room should be."

That night, when he finally tired himself out and climbed into bed with her, passing out almost immediately, she reached over and felt his skin. Hard, husky. It felt almost like wood. And when he got up in the morning, he left behind a pile of leaves beneath the sheets.

9

Saturday night was barbeque night here on Sycamore Lane.

We cooked hotdogs and hamburgers. We had on our Hawaiian shirts and khaki shorts. We wore our floral-printed sundresses and white frilly aprons. We sat on the patio and slurped shitty beer from dark amber bottles and we talked about professional sports and projects at work and what a "bang-up job" the local government is doing. We comment incessantly about the stupid fucking goddamn weather.

Brad Flatly and his wife Jennifer would come over. A big bowl of potato salad in Jennifer's hands. Brad holding a six-pack of watery domestic.

"Ding dong, neighborinos," Brad would say with a ceramic smile as he peeked his head around the side of the house. Harrison and Tabitha would be in the backyard, smiling ceramic smiles back at them.

Three hours later and Brad would polish off his last beer and yawn, raising his arms high into the air, making a big display of it like he just crossed the finish line at the Tour de France, and he'd say something stupid like "I think it's about time to hit the ol' sack, whadaya say, hun?"

And Jennifer would absentmindedly nod and say something to Tabitha like "Thanks for the lovely evening."

And then they would leave.

On Sunday, we would mow our lawns.

By Monday we're back on the bus downtown, on our way to work.

But that was before the hole.

Now the burgers sizzled on the grill, going from medium rare to well done as both Brad and Jennifer Flatly confusedly watched their deranged neighbor toss clump after clump of cold, wet sod over his weary shoulder.

"So what's the deal?" Brad eventually said. "You guys getting a pool or something?"

"Oooh, we should get a pool, Brad," said Jennifer "You know how long I've wanted a pool?"

"She's wanted a pool for a long time," Brad chuckled. "Next renovation, sweetie. I promise. Maybe we can even get Harrison to dig it for us, since he seems so dedicated to this little...hobby here. I mean, I love you darling, but *I'm* not about to chop my hands off and replace them with shovels. By the way, Harrison, are those—um—permanent modifications?"

The skin had grown over the handle of the trowel, fusing to it. Pinched flesh, red and green and raw, weaved its way through the fibers of the wood so that besides the metal end of the trowel's blade you couldn't tell where the shovel began.

"Do I look like I'm fucking around, Brad?" said Harrison.

"You totally got us," Tabitha quickly interrupted her husband. "We weren't going to mention it before, but Harry is so excited he just seems to want to...work on it all day, every day. I mean, why else would someone be digging a hole like this in the backyard, if not to install a pool?"

Harrison stopped and glared up at his wife.

"What are you doing, Tabitha?"

"What?" she said.

"Why are you lying to them?"

Tabitha laughed awkwardly. "What are you talking about, darling?"

"This isn't a pool and you KNOW that."

"Honey, please," Tabitha said through a forced smile. "We have company over."

"Wait," said Brad. "If it isn't a pool, then what is it?"

Harrison stood there for a moment, silent, save for the sound of the crickets in the bushes and the hiss of the meat burning over the charcoal. Brad and Jennifer exchanged a puzzled glance. Harrison sighed as he anchored his shovelhand into the dirt and used it to pivot his body out of the hole. He stomped his way across the yard, past his uncomfortable wife, and up onto the patio. There he stood as (metaphorically) tall as the spleenfruit tree, towering over his two seated neighbors.

"Hey, Harry, I didn't mean to offend—"

"Didn't you ever want more?" Harrison cut him off, nostrils flared and teeth like millstones between his jaws.

"Har, c'mon man," Brad said, shifting clumsily in his seat. "What are you talking about?"

"Life," Harrison said, holding his arms out wide, gesturing to everything around him. "All of it."

"Did I ever want more *life*?" Brad Flatly asked. "I-I don't understand the question."

"You don't understand," Harrison scoffed. "Of course you don't understand. You're so wrapped up in…in this bullshit…this COMFORTABLE bullshit we've been sustaining ourselves on that you can't think of anything beyond it. It's just a puppet show. A facsimile of happiness. We fill ourselves with these empty calories and act like it's our dessert. Is this it? Is this all there is? Just tell me, Brad, when you sleep at night, when you dream, what do you see?"

"Wha–what?"

"It's blackness, isn't it?"

There was a rumble. Like the roar of distant thunder, except it was coming from underneath their feet. Vibrations cast upwards, through the ground. Clumps of dirt shifted and slid. Almost imperceptible at first, but steadily growing in intensity. Soon, the whole yard churned like an upset stomach.

"Blackness?" said Brad.

"Blackness. Emptiness. A trench the size of eternity, filled up by nothing. Sleep bookended only by these flaccid and Xeroxed days; this consciousness like an albatross around your neck. Like a noose. You don't dream anymore, do you, Brad?"

Brad swallowed hard as he struggled to find his voice.

"No," he was finally able to mutter. "No, I don't dream."

Harrison leaned in close now, so that his mouth was right next to Brad Flatly's ear. Brad could feel his neighbor's hot breath against the hairs on the back of his neck. The rumbling from beneath the ground got even louder. Like feedback through a bass amp.

"You're already under the dirt and you don't know it," Harrison growled though his teeth. "We're ALL already under the dirt. And we're screaming to get out. Those are our voices, down there. Our ghosts. Screaming for help. But we shut our ears. We don't want to listen. We fill our lives with every useless distraction we can find an' we act like we won something. But not me, Brad. Not anymore. I swallowed the seed. I reached downward and opened the door. I can hear us."

"Harrison, stop it!" Tabitha reached out and laid her hand on her husband's shoulder. "These are our friends..."

"They are not my friends," Harrison replied as he spun around to face her. "They are just the people who happened to live in the house next to ours. They're no more my friends than the suit I wear to work is my skin."

The whole yard shook harder. A tremor. A seism. An epileptic seizure. The windows on the house rattled. Empty beer bottles trembled their way across the top of the polyglass table before plummeting over the edge. They shattered against the stone patio. The dirt in the hole shook. Seemed to boil. The low rumble escalating into a roar.

"I think we should really be going now," Brad said as he slipped sideways out of his chair and grabbed Jennifer by the wrist.

"And what about you, Tabitha?" said Harrison, turning his attention to his wife. "What lurks inside the darkness that fills you? When you sleep, what do you dream of?"

"Harry, this is NOT the time to be talking about this."

"Thank you for the lovely evening," Brad called out. His voice wavered uneasily, though he still felt the need to remain dogmatically congenial, painfully gracious, begrudgingly polite, smiling like it was the only thing he knew how to do, like a ventriloquist dummy at the precipice of some relentless and all-encompassing cosmic horror, as the earthquake forced a river of worms up through the dirt in the hole. These were the very same worms that greeted Harrison on the night he started to dig. And once again, they were suddenly everywhere. They filled up the hole like spaghetti in a pasta strainer. Squeezed in from all direction. They piled on top of one another, two inches deep.

The entire crater was alive. It was reaching towards the sky.

* * *

Brad and Jennifer scuttled towards the side of the house. They shuffled their feet in unison, step by careful step, but the ground was quickly eroding all around them, faster than they could move. The hole was growing exponentially. It was eating itself. And before Brad and Jennifer Flatly even realized it had happened, the hole had grown all around them. They were already inside of it.

The worms writhed around their feet. Moving in a frenzy, a slithering mass of hungry, wet mush. Jennifer was breathing heavily. In and out through her flared nostrils. Eyes wide with disgust.

She and her husband clung to each other like trash in an ocean gyre.

"Brad?" Jennifer eked, as the worms slithered and surged.

"It's okay, Jen. Stay calm. We can just…climb out…"

He reached over to the side of hole and attempted to pull himself up. The moist clump of soil immediately broke loose in his hand as another thick deluge of worms streamed out of the wall. Like a waterfall they poured, right into Brad Flatly's face. He went to scream but the worms filled up his mouth. Filled up his throat. Filled up his stomach. Filled up his whole body.

He flailed around, cartoonishly waving his arms up and down like a flightless bird, unable to breathe as the worms bore their way through the lining of his lungs. Crimson tears ran from his eyes and nose and dripped like jelly out of his ears. And then he slipped. He landed on his side in the puddle of wiggling, ravenous sludge. Jennifer yelped as she dropped to her knees next to her injured husband.

"Get up, Brad! Get up!"

Red, bloody welts were forming all over Brad's skin. The worms were biting into him. Swarming around him as tight as a mummy's cloth, ripping chunks of flesh off his body as they went. The sound of sticky mouths chewing. Tiny stomachs digesting. Miniature assholes shitting. He was being eaten alive.

Jennifer desperately scooped a handful of worms from Brad's ragged frame, but they stripped her hand of both muscle and meat before she could even toss them away. When she looked down, her legs too were already rendered into pink helves of bone, just the smallest globs of wobbling fat still attached to them. She couldn't stand up anymore. She couldn't run. Hungry and insatiable worms ravaged their way up her torso, organs spilling out of her yawning chest as the creatures parted the skin like the curtains of a stage.

No longer having the strength to keep herself upright, Jennifer collapsed. She too was on her side, face-to-face with her husband. Brad was almost a skeleton by now. The worms ripped him apart without respite. Without mercy. He looked like he was dissolving. Melting into the mire, becoming one with the ground.

His tired eyes rolled towards his wife.

"Brad, can you hear me still?" asked Jennifer.

"*Ggguhh*yess," he painfully burped.

She looked at her dying husband.

"I just wanted you to know, before we perish, that I never loved you," she said. "Never."

There was a moment where everything seemed still, where Jennifer's words registered in Brad's head. And then he reached out, pulled her close, embraced her. What was left of his cheeks perked up, forcing the slaughterhouse of his face into what could only be interpreted as a smile.

"I – neeeverr – *luughhh*loved – you – eitherrrr," he said back to her.

And then they were both consumed. Turned into dirt. Not even bones were left in their wake.

The worms retreated back into the soil.

Even though the worms were gone, the thunder growing from under the ground did not stop. The backyard still bellowed. The world still shook. The hole was not sated. It still grew deeper. Wider. Hungrier.

"If now is not the time to talk about this, then when is?" Harrison asked his wife, unabated. "When do we stop running? Stop pretending that tomorrow is some kind of concrete bunker for us to hide in instead of the bomb that's about to go off in our faces? When do we finally admit that things aren't perfect? That they were never perfect? That they're only getting worse?"

The spleenfruit tree rocked, swayed like a massive pompom back and forth as the ground underneath it loosened. For the first time since the backyard started collapsing in on itself, Tabitha looked around. She blinked skeptically, though it did nothing to erase the scene unfolding before her. She turned to Harrison for an explanation, but he too seemed to just be realizing how violent the world around them had quickly turned.

The ground quaked and they both nearly lost their balance.

"Harry, what is happening?" she nervously asked.

"I don't control this," he said as he found his footing and made his way so that he was standing next to his wife. "It's bigger than me."

They looked down in the hole and the bottom of it suddenly fell away. It was like it were yanked by an invisible hand, something reaching its way up through the mud to peel back the earth like an old bandage. The ground fell apart in long strips, leaving a gaping black chasm, an impossibly deep pit, in its place. There was no longer a backyard. There was only a bottomless hole.

The spleenfruit tree shook more. Uprooted. The ground was too weak, not thick enough to anchor its heavy trunk anymore. The tree jolted forward, falling towards the house that Tabitha and Harrison shared. It hit the roof first, splitting it in two, sending shingles and splinters to the churning sky. The tree continued to fall, cutting through the bedroom and living room, foyer and bath. Aluminum siding exploded out from the sides, bending and breaking. The house looked as if had been stepped on by a giant as the spleenfruit tree slammed sideways against the dirt.

Tabitha said, "Everything is falling apart."

Indeed, the entire neighborhood seemed to be suffering a fate similar to the Moss' backyard. And beyond the meager orbit of Brad and Tabitha, the entire city was under siege. Thunder and lightning filled the atmosphere as the ground below it churned in a maelstrom, sinking skyscrapers, consuming everything. Distant screams disappeared in the wind.

"There's only one place left to go," Harrison said.

"Where? What? What are we supposed to do?" Tabitha said through salty tears.

Harrison took a deep breath and stepped up next to his wife. He held out his rakehand – bent metal prongs for fingers spread open towards her. She too was breathing heavy. Chest pushing in and out. Fear had contorted her once-beautiful face into a funhouse vestige of itself. Confusion. Anger.

She looked at Harrison's hand like it was toxic. And, were the situation different, it *would* be toxic. His touch had been toxic for so fucking long, she could've touched him and died instantly.

But instead:

Her gaze drifted up. Met his eyes. There was something desperate in the way he was looking at her. Something real. Something vital. At first, off-putting, like it were a trap. But then she recognized the fear in his face too. A mirror of her own. He wasn't trying to beguile her. To trick her. In this moment, perhaps too little too late, he was trying to save her. For better or worse, what else could she do?

"I don't know about this…" she said.

"I don't either…" he replied.

She took his hand.

And into the hole they leapt.

"There's a rumblin' groan down below
There's a big dark town, it's a place that I've found
There's a world going on underground"

—Tom Waits, *Underground*

PART TWO
BELOW

10

Tabitha woke up.

At least, she thought she woke up. It was difficult to tell. Her mind was murky. Her muscles were sore. And the darkness that surrounded her was so total and all-consuming that it was difficult for her to know where the space around her ended and her body began. Were it not for the stream of adrenaline that was coursing through her veins, she might've evaporated, lost herself, completely. Instead, it was like her blood was jet fuel, screaming *good goddam morning, Tabitha Moss!*

She jolted upright. The boat she was in rocked back and forth.

So she was in a boat.

She didn't know that before, but she knew it now.

Her balance floundered as the wake around her swelled. She nestled in tighter, between the small craft's wooden ribs. She heard the waves lapping against its hollow sides; felt the warm, misty spray as they broke against the hull. All that, and yet she couldn't see them. Couldn't see anything. Couldn't see the water, but she knew it was there. Knew it was all around her. On all sides. As big as an ocean. She could feel its bigness.

"Ughhhh," a groan suddenly cut through the blackness. Tabitha clutched the edges of her rowboat and listened. Phlegmy lungs inhaled and exhaled, slowly. Almost a snore. Like a katydid in the night. And then she could smell him. His night sweat, that vile scent he would carry into their bed, wafting across the endless tide.

"Harrison?" Tabitha said. "Harrison is that you?"

"Tab-Tabitha?" he said.

"Shhhh! Keep your voice down!" she said.

"What? Why?"

There was a pause.

"Huh? Well I don't know why," she replied, no longer whispering. "Nevermind, I guess."

"What happened?" he said.

"What do you mean *what happened*?" she said. "You tell me!"

She heard him sitting up. Moving around. He was not in her boat, but he was nearby. Somewhere out there, she presumed, in a vessel of his own. Her own boat rocked softly, but the water around them was mostly calm.

"Where are we?" she asked.

"It's really dark in here," he replied.

"It's pitch black," she said. "I can't see a goddamn thing."

"And it's really quiet too…"

"Are you ignoring my question?"

"I mean, like, REALLY quiet…"

He fell silent. Tabitha couldn't even hear him breathing anymore. And then he shouted: "I don't hear them!" And his voice might as well have been a bomb going off for how much it startled his wife.

"Jee-zus, you almost gave me a heart attack. What are you talking about?"

"The voices," he said. "The ones in my head. I don't hear them anymore. The voices are gone."

"I don't care about that! Where the hell are we, Harrison?"

"Tabs, you really don't remember? We're in the hole. Everything was falling apart and we both leapt into the hole."

They lapsed back into silence.

"Are you there?" Harrison asked.

"What the FUCK?!" Tabitha screamed, loud enough to send ripples across the surface of the water. You could hear tiny waves *flipp-flipp-flippping* against each other. Hear the creak and groan of their rocking dinghies.

And then there was something else in the water too. Something splashing in the distance. Slowly coming their way.

"Hey, clam down. Do you hear that? What is it? What is that sound?"

"Calm down? CALM DOWN?! Are you *kidding* me?!?"

"I'm sayin' just be careful, okay? We don't know what's out there."

"Careful?!" she scoffed. "You're telling me to be careful? That's rich. That's a fucking laugh riot, Harrison. Careful, after you destroyed the whole yard? Destroyed the entire neighborhood? Destroyed everything we ever had with that stupid fucking goddamn hole?"

"Don't even start on me with this shit right now, Tabitha," he said. "I didn't destroy anything, okay? You saw it yourself. The ground just collapsed in on itself. It was like the hole reached up and yanked itself away from us."

"You were the one who was digging it!" she shouted into the darkness. The splashing in the distance was getting closer now. Their boats both pitched. Up and down. Side to side. It was big, whatever it was. And it was moving quickly in their direction. "You lost your fucking mind. You cut off your HANDS, for Christ's sake. You're the one who decided to go sifting through the dirt. I didn't ask for any of this, Harry. I didn't want to come down here."

"*Down here* was the only place left to go!" he shouted back. "If I hadn'ta pulled you down into the hole, who knows what would've happened. You coulda been trapped in the rubble of our house. It coulda collapsed all around you and left you crucified to the ground by pieces of plywood, driven through your limbs like nails, layin' there like a martyr to your shitty refusal to move."

"Oh yeah? Well, maybe I woulda been fine and it woulda been *your* head that woulda been crushed," Tabitha said. "Splattered by a 2x4 as the walls caved in around you. Brains like a Pollack painting all over the kitchen floor. I woulda taken your linoleum-splattered-brains and sold 'em to a museum. People would call me a genius; a goddamn art prodigy. I woulda moved to the city and met a handsome European man in his late 20s and I woulda let him fuck me in an alleyway behind a Chinese restaurant, near the dumpster, among the cats and rats, and as I quivered and came, I would've forgotten your name, forever."

The splashing grew louder. The boats rocked harder.

"You coulda been struck by a support beam, right in the stomach," Harrison gleefully said. "Driven like a battering ram into that paunchy belly of yours. You'da puked up your guts; intestines dribbling all outta your mouth like regurgitated scrambled eggs. You wouldn'ta died from the impact though. That'd be too easy. You woulda been trapped beneath the debris, face down in a puddle of your slop, forced to eat your own guts, eating your own half-digested shit, over and over and over again, until malnutrition finally overcame you."

Splashing so intense Tabitha had to shout as loud as she could.

"You coulda...you coulda fucking died a decade ago, long before we ever got here. I've fantasized about it so many times, you have no idea: What you would look like, in your coffin. All calm and cold and blue. I'd paint that spare room the same shade of blue as your dead face. Or even further back: You could've died before you met me. You could've saved me the pain of having to know you in the first place. To live with you. The pain of having to fall in...love. Goddamn it, were we ever in love, Harry? Is this the end result? Is love like everything else in this godforsaken universe, a seed that blossoms, only to wither and rot?"

"Wait..." said Harrison, his voice suddenly falling flat, grave.

"Wait what?" said Tabitha.

"Do you hear that?"

"Hear what?"

"The splashing from before, that was getting louder..."

"No, I don't hear anything."

"Me neither. Where did it go?"

The splashing had completely disappeared and the silence that replaced it was eerie. The kind of silence that seemed to not only be absent of sound, but absorb it. Had they kept screaming, the silence would've sucked it all up anyway.

"Are we safe?" Tabitha quietly asked.

But before Harrison had a chance to answer, the water beneath his boat suddenly exploded upward. It was as if a landmine had gone off. Tabitha fell backwards, landing hard on her back on the bottom of her raft. She yelped the oxygen out of her lungs. Pain like a thousand snakebites shot up her spine.

* * *

The splashing was back and now it was deafening. It filled up the air, thicker than the darkness itself.

"No!" she heard Harrison weakly scream, his voice almost consumed by the surrounding noise: a monstrous growl, wood being splintered as his boat cracked in half, his body hitting the water, immediately blending in with the rest of the commotion, just another *plink* in the torrent of *plinks*.

"Harrison?!" Tabitha shouted. "Harrison, what's out there?!"

At first he couldn't answer. Liquid had filled up his lungs. And the thing that had torn his rowboat apart was circling him, its tail slapping violently as it cut through the black water. Tabitha could hear it as it orbited her boat too, moving in a figure 8.

"Tabs!" he gasped as he bobbed up and down. "Help me!"

"Where are you?"

"This shovel and rake – I can't swim with these hands."

The creature bellowed. Deep and foreboding.

"I can't," she said, hugging her legs on the in the bottom of her rowboat, "I can't see anything."

"Fuc – k – I – can – 't – brea – the–"

Tabitha closed her eyes and exhaled. Her body felt incandescent, full of the wrong kind of energy. Like she had swallowed a dozen lightbulbs, glass and all. She felt like a transformer ready to explode.

"Harrison…?"

He didn't reply. He couldn't. His head was below the surface. The thing in the darkness went under too, after him, falling quiet as it cut through the water like the rudder of a ship.

"Harrison…?" Tabitha said again.

Silence and darkness so pervasive it was as if nothingness was all there ever was. Terrifying and empty. Helpless and alone. How many times, when she was lying in bed at night, had she wished this fate on her husband? Fantasized about violence on him as if he was a goddamn cartoon character: explode him with a stick of dynamite, run him over with a train, drop a wrought-iron anvil on his unsuspecting head. Whatever it took to get rid of him. But he'd always be back in the next scene. That's how cartoons worked. He'd always be okay.

But now he was gone. For real. And she was alone.

Still, this was what he wanted, wasn't it? This was all *his* fault, after all, not hers. She was blameless. She was an angel. He dragged her into this hole. She didn't MAKE him dig it.

Right?

RIGHT?!???

"Goddamn it," she mumbled to herself.

And then she leapt out of the boat, into the water.

Only it wasn't water she landed in.

What was it?

It was liquid, for sure. And it was wet. It was water-*ish*. But heavier. More viscous. Stickier. It was warm and syrupy and it was hard to move through, but she windmilled her arms in wide, lopping circles and swam towards where she had heard her husband dip under.

And then she felt it against her leg. This…creature. This sea monster. Whatever it was. It brushed up against her skin. She could feel its bumpy scales, slightly cooler than the ocean in which they swam. There was a give to it, like pushing against an inflated balloon. And the thing was long. Like, really long. It touched her and kept touching her as it dove down, down, down into the brine, touching her still. It must've been 60 feet, if she were sober enough to fathom a guess, but as it were, the thing seemed to go on forever.

Tabitha wanted to cry, but the rusty syrup caked up her eyes and filled her nose and mouth. The taste of metal, like sucking on a penny, that copper sting she could feel in her teeth.

She breathed in. Deep. Filling up her lungs with as much air as she could. And then she dove under too.

Were this book adapted into a screenplay, and were that screenplay turned into a movie, and were you in the theater watching that movie right now, this next scene would play out as thus:

The screen would be black. There would be no sound. You'd be sitting in your chair in the center of the back row, shifting around awkwardly in your padded seat, wondering just how long this blank screen was going to last. As it turns out, it's going to last a REALLY

LONG TIME, because the longer the filmmakers forced you to look at it, the more uncomfortable you became, and *that* was the exact emotion that they (and I) were going for. So this vague-sorta-discomfort settles around you like the mist around a coastal town, and now you're starting to realize just how peculiar this whole situation is: not just the soundless black celluloid flittering by in front of you, but to be here, in this room, with all these other people around you, these *strangers*. How did you get here? And now, you don't even want to breathe because you're afraid it's going to be too loud and everyone is going to turn around and give you that look like HOW DARE YOU RUIN THIS DRAMATIC SILENCE BY BREATHING SO LOUDLY.

As Tabitha went under the water, it felt exactly like *that*. Except in the book version it lasted longer than it would on screen. It lasted for the longest amount of time you could possibly conceive of. This isn't a movie, and the length of time that passed here is completely up to you and your imagination. How deep does it go? If you imagine her under the water for 5000 years, then she was under there for 5000 years. If it was for the rest of eternity, she was under until eternity passed.

And then, after that interminable amount of time later:

She emerged.

Tabitha breached the surface like a buoy in a storm. Screaming, gasping, greedily pulling air into her lungs. And Harrison was in her arms. Limp. Not breathing.

Up ahead, there was a light. The first light that she had seen since they woke up in this ocean at the bottom of the hole. It didn't shine like headlights or flicker like a candle. It was subtle and soft, illuminating a ceiling high overhead along thick, wet ridges. This was no dawn. This was a light from below.

And the water stirred.

Like a whirlpool, the water stirred.

The sea creature was beneath her now. She thought she felt it, like a phantom, brushing against the bottoms of her feet. Over and over, teasing its arrival, hinting at something the way a stiff breeze might portend a coming storm. It teased until the thing *actually* brushed against her feet. Firm and fast and very, very REAL.

Its back bucked up out of the water, capsizing her boat. The dinghy went stern up, then sank straight to the bottom as fast as a boulder. There was nothing for her to grab onto. Nothing left afloat.

Tabitha wrapped her arm around her husband tighter, locking her fingers around the front of his chest though she could barely stay above the surface herself. And she swam.

In the lowlight, she could make out the shape of the beast. Cylindrical, like a tube, with one end slightly fatter than the other. For its size, it moved with grace, sleek and eel-like, quickly cutting towards her and her unconscious husband.

Tabitha paddled furiously. Kicking. Fighting to move forward. Her husband was an anchor affixed to her side. The monster getting closer. And then even closer. She didn't know where she was going. She didn't know if there was even anywhere left to go.

The beast behind her roared.

Uncertain light refracted off the water's surface, casting dark shadows across the sanguine sea.

She looked behind her and could see the head of it, rising up. The mouth opened. There were no teeth inside, but like a suction it pulled ocean into its maw. The roar she had been hearing she now recognized as the sound of air being torn asunder as it was sucked into this giant worm's pharynx, down its esophagus, to the gizzard whirling like a garbage disposal.

Up ahead, a luminescent shore appeared. Not shining, but lit up by an impossible light, emanating from nowhere. To call it light would be a misnomer, and yet, it gave shape to the darkness as if it were molding clay. There was shore. She could see it. And then she looked down. This water, this liquid she was swimming in, it was not water at all.

It was blood. An ocean of blood.

She reached the bank on a wave of viscera. Guts and slime and chum soaking through her clothes. She and Harrison washed up on the beach like whales. She sputtered as she lay him on his back beneath her. Gore splashed at their feet.

The worm behind them rose up, a living pipe of intestine, a

fleshy skyscraper just inches from the roof of this quivering cave.

"Wake up," she said to her comatose husband, shaking him by the shoulders, slapping him in the face. "Goddamn, Harry, you moron. Wake-the-fuck-up!"

The worm started forward. Like a tree, falling. Slowly at first, letting gravity do most of the work, its mouth open, its stomach hungry, digestive juices sloshing, dripping, grinding.

"Harry," she cried, shaking him so hard now his head slammed against the ground.

"Fuck you for doing this to me!" she screamed to her husband and the worm and existence in general. "Fuck you! Fuck you! FUCK YOU!"

The lips of the worm closing in around them. And then:

"What?" said a groggy Harrison Moss, his eyes fluttering open.

Tabitha let out a relieved sigh which barely escaped from her parted lips before it got tangled up in a conflicted smile. The full range of human emotions lay trapped on her face like flies in a spider web. She was happy and angry and sad in equal measures. And then, the fear. Oh yes, THE FEAR. The fear took over. She screamed, remembering the giant worm behind them, hungry mouth open as wide as a planet, about to swallow them both. But when she turned and looked, the monster was gone, completely vanished with no trace, save for the sound of small ripples of blood lapping against the banks on which they lie.

11

It wasn't exactly a sun and it wasn't exactly a sky, but it was light nonetheless, and it filled up the air above them like the ceiling of this cave was the horizon at dusk. The surrounding walls were so high and wide that they didn't appear to be walls at all. It was like a cloudy evening, orange and pink and dark in places where the shadows of night abutted up against each other, but the overall color was calm and the cave felt no more like a cave than the sky around the Earth felt like a glass dome.

They walked away from the ocean slowly, across the beach like zombies, like lost little children. The ground crunched beneath their feet.

"Where are we going?" Tabitha asked, without looking up.

"Forward," Harrison replied.

And forward they went.

They left footprints across the powdery white grain like they were slogging across the surface of the moon. Tabitha stopped and reached down, scooping up a handful of it. She let it run through her fingers, like an hourglass.

"This isn't sand," she said.

"No," Harrison agreed, inspecting it closer himself. "It's bone."

"Bone dust?"

"The water appears to be blood and land is made of bones," he nodded.

"But why?" asked Tabitha.

"I don't know," Harrison replied. "It's like they've been digested."

"Chewed up and spit out," she said. "Probably by that...sea worm thing."

"I guess not everyone makes it out of that ocean alive..."

And they continued on.

The further from the shore they got, the bigger the bone fragments became. Granules became barbed chunks, before the two of them found themselves surround by femurs and skulls, festooned about. Complete skeletons stacked in piles or sprawled on top of one another like they had died, rotted, and were vulture-picked clean as they attempted to claw away.

The land descended along a gradual slope. The ocean rested above the beach, defying gravity in an impossible way. The blood should've run downward. But it didn't.

The hill funneled forward, towards a singular point. At least a mile away, still, but this cave was not endless. Tabitha squinted. It appeared to be some kind of flat surface. Perhaps there was a way out, cut into the rock? It was still too far away for the two of them to make out in much detail, barring the fire-licks of nearby torches.

Regardless, from here on out, it was the only way to go.

12

Tabitha and Harrison slowly trudged through dust and bone, the skeletons getting more and more complete as they went. Some had random bits of flesh still attached, chunks of red meat wrapped around them like unfinished steak. Others were fresher, and didn't appear injured all, aside from a few swollen purple cuts and distended bruises. A little bit of makeup and they'd be coffin-ready. It'd look like they were sleeping.

And then, just a little bit farther down from that, the bodies stopped being dead at all. They were awake. Alive. Or rather, alive-*ish*. Harrison and Tabitha walked on top of living people packed so tightly they had become enmeshed, as if they were one giant field of skin, melded into each other. A carpet of flesh. Fingers sprung up like saplings, hair like patches of overgrown grass. Worms wriggled in and out of nostril holes.

The eyes under their feet watched the two of them disapprovingly. Mouths gurgled incoherently.

"They're people," Tabitha said. "Just regular people, sewn into the landscape."

A tongue came out of a mouth and licked at her feet.

"Are they dead?" she asked.

"Some of them appear to be," he replied.

"Can we help them?" she said.

"I think it's too late," he said back to her.

The smell was horrendous. It was warm and wet and everywhere. And then they couldn't walk forward any further because they had arrived at the bottom of the hill, at a wall.

The wall spread out like wings, from one horizon to the next, a rampart so high that it was impossible to see past it. Along the top, torches burned. Halos of orange light melted down the battlement. The glow of the fire mixed with the glow of the cave itself. The two lights smeared together like paint on a palette.

"Oh man, my stomach still hurts," said Harrison, pulling a handful of leaves out of his mouth and tossing them aside. The sweat on his forehead was tinted green.

And then there was a gate. A towering gate, arched like the one that held back Kong on Skull Island. It went up so high that it touched the top of the cave, was built into it.

The two of them stepped up to it and stopped. Harrison tried the handle, but it didn't budge.

"We can't go any further," he said. "It's sealed shut."

Tabitha pounded her fist against the door. It echoed through the chamber, the sounds bouncing around before fading away behind them like mocking laughter. She pounded again, and again, and again, until her fist hurt. Not even a rattle from beyond the gate. Her knocking was answered by nothing.

She let her hand lay against the wood. Breathing hard. Exhausted.

"Tabitha?" Harrison said softly, reaching out before realizing his hand was still a shovel and pulling it back away.

She turned to him. Tears filled her eyes.

"I don't want to be with you anymore," she said. Her voice trembled as she spoke.

"What?"

"I don't want to be with you," she said again, this time more definitively. "This isn't what I signed up for. I don't want to be in this marriage anymore."

"I know," he solemnly said. "But this isn't a mistake. It *can't* be a mistake. We're not down here by accident. The voices called out for you and I. This was going to happen to us, sooner or later."

"They called out to *YOU*, Harrison. I didn't hear anything," she said. "Now, how do we open this door? How do we get back to the surface? How do we get out of here?"

"The ground gave way. Right beneath us. It fell through, and we fell with it."

Tabitha pushed against the giant gate, inspected its hinges, searched in vain for some kind of release mechanism.

"Locked. Solid. Could we smash through it?" she asked.

"We deserve this," he said. "Can't you see that? We deserve to be buried alive."

She turned around and glared at him. Silence followed, and suddenly, the cave seemed too small. Like it could barely fit the two of them.

"What were we supposed to do?" Tabitha asked.

At first he didn't answer. He looked down at his mutant hands and then raised back his gaze, locking eyes with his wearied wife.

"I don't know anymore," he finally said.

And, as if he had just spoken the 'magic word,' like *open sesame*, the torch flames flickered and the gate creaked.

It split down the middle and the two doors parted.

13

Harrison and Tabitha Moss passed through the entrance, unsure of who or what to expect on the other side.

They found themselves on a cobblestone street in the middle of the night, somewhere on the perimeter of an unfamiliar city.

Jagged apartment buildings sat on either side of them, decaying and baroque, unevenly placed like the teeth in a neglected mouth.

These buildings lined the intersecting avenues, creating somewhat of a tunnel effect, blocking most of their periphery. Sallow light filled the windows of some of the apartments. There were sounds coming from inside, raspy and rustling, not voices in the traditional sense, but whispered nonetheless, and a breeze that was not uninviting, causing summertime curtains to dance their way into the adjacent alleys.

The gate slowly shut behind them and locked itself with a loud, metallic clank. The noise was so jarring against the hushed murmur coming from the nearby buildings that a spooked Tabitha quickly spun around on her heel to greet it. There, she saw no door at all. It was sealed up tight, the opening waxed over like an old scar. Like the vagina she once had.

The wall behind them stretched up until it blended into the evening sky, spilling upward, to become just more wall. She ran her hand against it. Smooth, cold, impassible. Is this some sort of second cave they were in? A cave within the cave? Was the last room just an antechamber? It sure seemed that way, but how could this second cave be bigger than the one that surrounded it? Were they still trapped? There didn't appear to be any obvious way to egress, and yet, they didn't really feel trapped at all. The unfamiliar city was wide open in front of them. A big as any city they've ever known. They had gone down into the hole, hadn't they? They were still inside the Earth, weren't they? They were here, in this kingdom of bone and dirt – and so, Tabitha wondered, what was this moon that shone above them? Because it was there, high above, white and round, like the moon she thought she knew. Was this a false moon? A pseudo moon? A ball of pale light masquerading as a moon? Did this imposter even know what it took to be a moon? Did it know what a moon *means* when it rises up, full and pregnant? Did it know how to steer ships?

For that matter, did Tabitha know what a moon means? Did Harrison?

Do you?

Up ahead, a vision of downtown faded into view.

Skyscrapers lined up, lit up. Squares of concrete against the ashen horizon. But more than just the buildings themselves, there also appeared to be a volcano sticking up in the center of the metropolis. Steep on the sides, yet shorn on the top, it dwarfed the meager structures built around it by hundreds of feet. It was almost as if the city itself were built in reverence of this massive mountain. Like the buildings were just worshipers genuflecting at its feet.

From the upper basin of the volcano there flickered an orange light. A fire light. This appeared to be what illuminated the city and refracted off the "moon." Steam rose from the crater in puffs, creating an ambient fog that hung over the cityscape like a wedding veil. This was not a skyline either of them recognized. This wasn't Albany or Dayton. This wasn't LA or Chicago or San Antonio, Texas. This certainly wasn't motherfucking New York City. They were somewhere else entirely.

"I got a feelin' we're not in Kansas anymore," said Harrison.

Tabitha whipped her head around and sneered at him.

"Why would you say that?"

"Huh?"

"That stupid clichéd phrase, about Kansas," she said. "That thing from *The Wizard of Oz.*"

"Ah jeez, I dunno," Harrison shrugged. "I thought that was the thing people are suppose'ta say in situations like this."

Tabitha sighed and walked down the road.

"Whoa wait," Harrison said. "Where are you going?"

"Where else would I be going, Harry? I'm getting out of this fucking hole. I'm gonna find a way back up. I'm gonna go home."

He took a few steps after her.

"Hey, no, you can't do that," he said.

"Like hell I can't!" she said back.

"Tabitha, we don't know where we are. We don't know where home even is."

"It's certainly not here," she said.

They stood there staring at each other for a moment, like gunfighters at high-noon, each one waiting for the other to draw their weapon.

"You know I can't go with you," he eventually said. "If you walk away."

"I don't care," she said back.

"We're down here for a reason. The voices called to us. The shadows beckoned us."

"Jesus, not more of this mystic bullshit. You're like a broken record…"

"Look," he said. "We can either live on the precipice, forever in fear of falling over, or we can journey to the bottom of this and find out what it's all about. We're halfway there already. You know as well as I do that this story will end at some point, regardless of the paths we choose. So you just gotta stop and ask yourself this one question before it does: Do we have anything to gain by being here, Tabitha?"

She rolled her eyes.

"I don't have time for this," she said. "We were comfortable until you lost your fucking mind, Harrison. We had a house. A *life*. It may not have been perfect, but it was ours. And it's all gone now, so I'm not kowtowing to you any longer. I'm not following you around like a lost little puppy. I'm gonna find my way out of here and then I'm never coming back. Whatever *you* do is up to you."

"Well then…" he said, pausing for dramatic effect, "I guess this is goodbye?"

She scoffed and shook her tired head.

"You know, that's a cliché thing to say, too," she replied.

And she walked away, leaving Harrison standing there.

And the false stars twinkled.

And the fake moon shined.

14

She travelled down the road.

She didn't have a specific destination in mind, save for the vague notion of the "home" that had collapsed in their wake as the hole in the backyard had swallowed everything up. She certainly hadn't considered how to get out of this place, if there even was a way to get out of this place. The sky was built into the walls, like a snow globe. Solid rock. That didn't leave her with much hope of escaping anytime soon.

The volcano downtown grumbled and hissed, but other than that, this city was eerily quiet. No cars, no bikes, no pedestrians bustling to and fro like they would in the world above. There were streetlights casting yellow pyramids of light down to the pavement, and there was the shade that filled up all the spaces in between that, but even in the dark she didn't see anything out of sorts. Of course, a city street being as quiet as this was, in itself, already out of sorts.

And then:

She could hear footsteps behind her. Distant at first, but getting closer. Two footsteps for every one she took, reverberating off the cobblestone sidewalks and the concrete facades of the rotten buildings nearby.

clack Her heels said.

clack-clack The echo replied as it trailed her down the desolate street.

clack-clack Her heels doubled down as she quickened her pace.

clack-clack-clack-clack The darkness answered back.

At first it was merely repeating her, parroting her exactly, as echoes often do, a one-sided conversation between her and the wall. Repeating her, the echo was, until it spoke on its own. These were not her footsteps she was hearing. She was being followed.

"Hello?" she called out. "Harry, is that you?"

The clacking continued. Grew more feverish. Like a secretary typing on a keyboard. Like raindrops falling on a tin roof. Footsteps clacked on the pavement in quick succession, louder and fuller with every passing second.

Tabitha froze. Eyes darted. And yet, she couldn't see anyone. Fear overcame her, set her muscles to stone and her blood to ice. After escaping from the worm monster in the ocean of blood, with its ravenous maw set to grind her up and deposit her on the seashore with the rest of those hapless corpses, she hadn't the desire nor the strength to keep on running. She didn't ask for this life, and she didn't think it was fair that she had to keep atoning for it. Yet here she was, lost in a dark city, stalked from the shadows by a *clacking* whose goal is nebulous at best, and homicidal at worst.

Then, the thing that was following her came out from a nearby alley, and she saw it.

It was a beetle.

A massive rhinoceros beetle. The size of a box truck.

Its oil-black body glistened, like it was wet, reflecting back the lowlight of the counterfeit moon. Its barbed legs slapped against the street. *clack-clack-clack* Tabitha wanted to recoil, to scream, but she didn't. She didn't even skip a breath. She wasn't afraid at all. It was like her brain glitched and then rebooted itself, its operating system blank, ready to be reprogrammed. Something about this gigantic beetle barreling horn-first down the street seemed perfectly natural to her. No more remarkable than a Toyota Carolla.

In fact: she was more surprised by the fact that she wasn't surprised than she was by the human-sized worm riding on the beetle's back.

The worm pulled back on the beetle's antenna, which acted like reins, causing it to slow to a trot, and eventually stop. Tabitha stood there as the creature slid down the side of the beetle, leaving a trail of slime behind him, and settled there before her.

He was a very handsome worm.

Wait, what? Did Tabitha really just use the word *handsome* to describe a worm?

She tried to feel terror, wished to be repulsed, but those emotions just weren't there.

The Worm Man had a tuft of black hair, slicked back into a pompadour like a prince in a Disney cartoon. Other than that, there was no way to determine his top from his bottom, as he was just a tube of loosely connected pink flesh. He slunk up to her with confidence, as if he didn't know he was a worm at all. He coiled up, his body pulsating. He flexed.

She felt her skin become flush. She was blushing.

"Can you help me get home?" she asked The Worm Man.

He didn't say anything back to her. He couldn't. He had no voice box from which to speak. But somewhere, deep inside her head, she knew this Worm Man was answering her:

Yes.

He flattened out the top part of his body and motioned for her to climb with him onto the back of the beetle.

She awkwardly tried to bring a foot up onto the scarab's smooth shell, but couldn't find a stirrup. The Worm Man tossed back his hair and slid underneath her, bucking his back up, easily lifting her legs with the bulk of his body. She was able to grab onto one of the ridges that ran along the giant insect's spine and pull herself the rest of the way.

She sat on the beetle like a mahout on an elephant. The Worm Man slithered up behind her, his body sticky with mucous. He wrapped the front part of himself around the beetle's antenna and gave it a tug. It continued down the street as it had before.

clack-clack-clack

15

Did the sun rise underground?

There was certainly a moon, as I've already established. A big rock jammed into the ceiling, phosphorescent and blue.

But if there was no sun, then there was no morning, and if there was no morning, then there was no tomorrow. Under here, the night had usurped the day. Harrison didn't wear a wristwatch. He didn't even have wrists anymore, unless you count the infected bands of wet flesh that encircled the areas where the tools had replaced his hands. And even then, he might've thrown a watch around it had it not been for the thick, white roots growing out of the wounds instead. These roots twisted up around the stems of his hands, held them in place. He could feel the pressure of the seed growing inside him, pushing out against his skin, looking for places to go.

Harrison Moss had no wristwatch, and as such, couldn't tell the time proper, but he felt like he had been wandering around this subterranean city for days.

Days. Ha! I suppose we're going to need a new word for that if we're going to stay down here.

Occasionally he would spot some sort of insect scuttling by, darting out of an alley, past a streetlight, its shadow stretched out wide and crooked like it was running past a funhouse mirror. In the windows of the apartments, where the unintelligible whispering seemed to coalesce into a buzz, the sound of which reminded him of the chop saw running in the shed, he could see the shapes of bugs peeking up, peeking out, regarding him with disdain. Earthworms, mostly. The population of this place was overwhelmingly of the annelid variety. They were under the dirt after all, and if any creature held providence over such a place, then these nightcrawlers were certainly it.

He was a stranger in a strange land.

The strangest land.

The voices had stopped talking to him though. Stopped boring through his thoughts the way a worm would bore through the soil. He should be grateful for that, right?

With this newfound lucidity his hands now seemed almost comical. A shovel and a rake? C'mon! It was truly a bizarre thing to do, that much was clear, but the compulsion to dig had been so overwhelming at one point that Harrison thought that was all there was. He was a digging machine. An excavator. A tool himself —employed for purposes far grander and far more mysterious than he could ever hope to understand. If you asked a hammer what it thought the meaning of life was, would it be able to answer you? Of course not! How was he supposed to describe that to his beleaguered wife? And yet, now his hole was done, and he was left to aimlessly wander this odd city.

Even for the difficult sojourn he had steeled himself to go on, he hadn't considered where he would go once he got there.

Now, were this book one of those contrived kind of novels where the "indomitability of the human spirit" was to be the big takeaway in the end, Harrison's inner monologue (as read in the last section, above) would've been him realizing some cornball lesson about life being all about the "journey" and not the "destination," or that sort of *blah-blah-blah* nonsense.

Clearly, that is NOT what this book is about! If it were, this story would've ended when the hole in their backyard gave way and Harrison and Tabitha both fell in. Swallowed up and buried by their own hubris, the weight of which was the entire world; they both received their deliciously ironic finale. Roll the credits.

THE END.

Shit, in retrospect, that's probably where this story should've ended. That *was* the logical conclusion, after all. A clear and unpretentious metaphor. Poetic, too. What was left to say? What the fuck could possibly happen next?

Well, here's what the fuck happened next:

Harrison Moss heard music.

Yup, music.

Low and distant. The bass purring over an electronic drumbeat. It made the world vibrate, like the street itself were the string of a harpsicord.

Harrison walked towards the sound. It was almost as if he was being beckoned, as if these passing notes could reveal to him his new life's purpose. And perhaps they could. Who am I to say?

He tapped his shovel hand against the stem of each of the streetlights as he passed them, the metal against metal going **ping** each time.

ping ping ping

For the briefest of moments, he thought of Tabitha and how, at one point, *she* was the music by which he moved. But this thought was ephemeral – he didn't hold onto it, he didn't even attempt to, as the time for holding onto things had long since expired. He knew that without hands to aide him, holding onto things was now physically impossible too. Nonetheless, here was the shape his thoughts of Tabitha took:

He remembered how she used to like to dance. They both liked to dance. It was a thing they used to do together, when they were younger. He would take her out to a club downtown and they would sip vodka tonics and laugh and smile and talk about whatever floated through their minds, and they would relinquish themselves to the music, and to each other, and night would blend into this big and beautiful blur, a montage of jubilant and hopeful vignettes, one after another, glued together by feelings of safety and affection.

They'd go back to his apartment, their bodies still humming, and have sex in a drunken haze. It was magical.

Moments like that once seemed so important. So obvious. And, oddly enough, so easy to come by. Loving someone else had felt so natural to him then. He didn't even have to think about it. It felt like breathing. Automatic and effortless.

But love is not a wellspring. It's not just there for you to discover like a rowboat in the bloodiest of seas. Their love eventually ran out. Ran dry. It didn't last. And neither did the home they built. And neither did his hands. If there were love left to be wrought from this world, his wife was not the lens through which to look for it.

At the end of the road, nestled between two tall apartment buildings, was a warehouse of sorts. Its veneer was squat and plain. *Unassuming* is the word one could use to describe it. Or, it WOULD'VE been the word one could use to describe it, had the dance music not been growling from behind its walls. The rows upon rows of windows that lined the top of the building glowed in hues of indigo and pink, not bright colors, but deep, blending in with the brick so that the stone itself seemed to shine.

It was a club with no name. A warehouse rave. And in this underground city where it was always night, this was a party that had no end.

Outside the front doors, insects had gathered. Crickets, termites, cicadas, earwigs, and worms. The worms, up on their haunches, numbered in the hundreds, all of them standing about the height of Harrison himself, waiting in a line to enter the building.

Harrison passed them. The creatures with black marble eyes looked him with contempt. The blind, eyeless ones did their best to do the same.

Unsure of where to go and what to do, bereft of a purpose any loftier than this, he got in line behind them.

Arms crossed in front of his chest, he shifted uncomfortably as the insects around him clicked and chirped. He was pretty sure they were not communicating to each other. Or maybe they were. To him, they were just noises. Horrible noises.

The music was good, though. It was just like the music he and Tabitha used to dance too. Identical, in fact.

And then, interrupting the thoughts of Tabitha that once again flittered through his head, he noticed a lady worm sashaying past the line with a nod and a wiggle.

There were no distinguishing marks to denote her gender, of course, but he could just tell: the way her body curved, genteel and soft, a parabola of the most sensual and feminine design. He felt his blood quicken, force-feeding more oxygen to the sprouting seed within him. Leaves unfurled from his nostrils and he exhaled them out. Was she coming his way? Harrison let a smile slip across his lips as she slithered up next to him.

He ran his raked hand through his hair.

"What's…inside this building?" he asked, even though he already knew.

She coiled down, twisted her body in a loop around his arm as if she was his red carpet escort, and gave him a little tug. He seemed confused at first, his feet planted firmly to the ground, but she tugged again and soon he relinquished, let her lead him. They moved slowly. She wasn't rushing him. They walked forward, along the side of the line. He ignored the jealous glares from the impatiently waiting insects.

When they arrived at the front, a large, fat beetle guarded the door. They stopped. The music was louder here as it spilled through the opening. He looked them over, skeptically. Harrison gulped and raised his eyebrows. The Worm Woman cocked her head in a reprimanding manner. The beetle slid aside and let the two of them pass through the entrance, into the club.

16

The music was so loud it sounded like it was underwater. The bass was more of a feeling than an actual tone. Decibels bellowing either so low or so high they merely flirted with the edge of Harrison's perception. The whole building shook. The bugs inside it shook. Every molecule that made up Harrison's body shook too. It was a party.

Harrison smiled as The Worm Woman led him in further. Towards the dance floor.

They found a spot, nestled between the moist, cold bodies of the other insects. Harrison and The Worm Woman danced. He brushed his rake hand along the curve of her back as she ground up against him in time to the beat. She could feel the prongs, scraping against her mucusy skin. He could feel the clammy heat radiating from her sticky body; they were the only two creatures in this building who appeared to be warm. Wait, are worms capable of generating heat? How does that even work? DON'T GOOGLE THE ANSWER! It'll just ruin the mystery. This Worm Woman was certainly generating heat, and that's all that matters.

This was…this whole thing…it felt…like a dream.

Something about this reminded Harrison of the night he woke up and replaced his hands with gardening tools. It all seemed so far away to him now, as if it had happened to someone else, and he only watched. The screech of the rusty saw, the sensation of his hands getting chopped into little pieces – did it even hurt? – and even before that, there was the afternoon prior: Harrison in the backyard, on his hands and knees. Eating that seed from the spleenfruit tree. Swallowing it down. Letting it grow. Why did he eat that disgusting seed, anyway? There had to be a reason.

Right?

It was like it was someone else's memory trapped in his head. Like a photo album on his shelf that belonged to some neighbor he never met.

The beat sped up, doubled-timed, matching the tempo of his ever-accelerating heart. He continued to move and sweat on the dancefloor. Oh, but he loved it. In that moment, he surrendered himself completely. His feet, unencumbered. His spirit, free. A stupid smile on his stupid face, looking completely stupid and he danced stupidly in this den of bugs. THIS must've been why he dug the hole. THIS must've been what he was looking for.

And there, with the worm in front of him, now rubbing her backside up and down his torso, seductive and obscene. She was a monster – OF COURSE she was a monster – but he couldn't deny his attraction to her. He could feel it inside of him. Something growing. Spreading. Pushing against the inside of his skin, trying to claw its way out.

What was he then, if not a monster too?

She turned to face him, her wicked curves as beguiling as the beat of the music itself. He threw his head back, allowed her to rub him, tease him, arouse him, awaken him.

And after an indeterminable amount of time later, when he opened his eyes again, he saw that they were the only two still dancing.

That's odd, he thought.

The bass drum still crashed like Tectonic plates.

The music got swimmier.

And then it wasn't music at all, but a sustained hum. A protracted growl, almost seismic, as it buried itself deep into Harrison's marrow. This wasn't a song he heard, but a roar he felt from within.

They had been given a berth, a circle to move in all their own, and every other bug in the club was watching them. Hundreds of eyeballs all pointed their way. Dark clouds beneath glass domes, jammed into skulls of nightmare shapes; these were the eyes of salacious and alien voyeurs, and the insects were ready for a show.

Harrison's dancing slowed, though The Worm Woman kept whipping around like her body were a lasso.

"Wait…what's happening?" he said, though he might as well have not said anything at all, because if these insects understand English – and he had seen no indication to suggest that they could – they wouldn't have been able to hear him anyway.

The Worm Woman jerked her head around, a tremble of the short bristles that lined her sides, as she wrapped the lower half of her body around Harrison's feet, encircling him two or three times, up his body and around his chest.

"Wait a minute, I know you," he said to her, again, aloud in a room full of deaf ears. "I've seen you before. That night. The night I started to dig. You where there, in the shadows. In and out of my perception, like a ghost. You were in my house! Watching me. You had something to do with this, didn't you?" Now panicked, "What are you? What is happening here? Where have you brought me?"

And then she squeezed.

The breath shot right out of his mouth as she increased the pressure on his lungs. Squeezed tighter. His knees buckled and he toppled to the ground. She twisted up around his hands now, pining the shovel and rake to the dirt floor.

He tried to thrash, to kick free and run, but it was useless. He couldn't escape. And he knew it.

"What are you doing?" he muttered.

She pushed him down harder, laying her thick sausage-like body against his face so that he had to turn his head sideways to keep from suffocating completely.

She then stretched herself out as far as she could stretch, thinning into a long tube the thickness of a cucumber, her entire body growing until she is 25, then 30, then 35 feet from end to end. Living spaghetti. She took the tip of what would be her head, bulbed it up like an angry fist, and pushed her way past Harrison's lips, down his throat, deep inside, into his body.

17

Somewhere else, on the opposite end of the city, after what seemed like a week of endless travel (though, again, without the sunrise/sunset cycle, it was difficult to tell) a beetle the size of a box truck was skittering its way down a suburban street.

Tabitha rode on its back. The Worm Man sat in front of her. She wrapped her arms around the tube of his body. His skin was moist. She rested her cheek against his backside and felt safe.

The Worm Man steered the beetle around a corner. And as the street before them flattened out, Tabitha could see it terminated a few houses ahead of her, in a cul-de-sac. A dead end.

The trees that lined the sidewalk here were barren: thin wooden braches, leafless and naked. They looked like calcium-starved bones, like they were skeletons clawing for the ceiling. But still, something about this all seemed very familiar and Tabitha couldn't quite shake the feeling of déjà vu until she looked at the street sign identifying the road they were traveling down. It was falling over, covered in grime and hard to read, but she only needed to glimpse it in part to know exactly what it said:

Sycamore Lane.

This was her street.

And that decaying building up ahead? That was her house.

The Worm Man pulled the beetle into the driveway and slid down. He extended his body sideways to give Tabitha something to hold on to as she made her way down too.

He even opened the front door and let her into the house. He was a courteous worm.

She stepped through the entranceway and into the foyer.

It looked like her home inside. It was unmistakable: the architecture, the layout, even the furniture and decorations were in exactly the same places that Tabitha remembered them.

Yet…something was off. Her head swiveled back and forth. Where exactly *was* she?

The entire house – the entire neighborhood in fact – looked as if it had been abandoned, then spent the next decade falling further and further into a state of condemnation. Table and chairs, though seemingly rotten here, were the same table and chairs she had always known. The couch was a festering lump of soiled cloth. The rooms were gray, cobwebby, and quiet, and a thick layer of dirt covered everything. The walls creaked and cracked. The floorboards sighed mournfully under her feet.

Tabitha took it all in slowly, bulldozing a little mountain of dust as she ran her finger across the mantle, breathing the sarcophagus air of this dead living room.

She came upon a framed photograph. The edges of it had been eaten up by time, staining the rest of the picture yellow and brown. It was a wedding photo. Her wedding photo, to be precise. Tabitha in her dress, once white, now jaundiced as the film aged. Harrison standing behind her, tuxedo tie and suit coat on, but, for some reason, his face had been obscured. It was as if someone had tried to scrub it out with bleach. A white void in the photo, a hasty smudge: Tabitha and this empty smear of a man, joined in holy matrimony.

'Til death do them part.

She moved to the next set of pictures. It was them in their first apartment, when they still lived in the city, downtown. The place was a dump, roach-infested and full of mold, on the 6th floor of an apartment building that didn't even have an elevator. When they moved in, they had to drag the loveseat up the thin, crooked staircase and it had gotten stuck on the bend on the third floor. They sat there, sweaty and laughing, until the old guy who lived on the floor underneath came and helped force it through. His name was Mr. Humboldt. They ate peanut butter sandwiches that night because it was the only food they had. It wasn't that long ago, was it?

Those were the honeymoon days. The salad days. But now the photograph paper looked dozens of years older than it actually was, the colors faded, and Harrison's face bleached out. She went through all the pictures in the room, looking at the walls like a patron at a museum. She pulled a crumbling picture album from the bottom shelf of the bookcase and flipped through the pages. It was the same every time. He was gone, scratched out, whitewashed over. Like he was being erased.

"Harrison," she mumbled his name out loud to herself, the sound of it tingling like Ajax on her tongue. And then again. "Harrison." She said it again and again and again, until the word lost all meaning. "Harrison, Harrisan, Harridsin, Harrimstem, Harrrrddisstennnd."

And somewhere in the gray noise of her voice, in the ritualistic chanting of the nonsense word that his name had become, she also lost the image of his face. It was just like in the photos, but now in her mind's eye too. Like he got zapped from her memory. Poof! Smoke! Just like that. He was gone.

But it wasn't empty space that replaced him. There was a figure there, yes, taking up his place in her brain, but the figure was ill-defined. She stood in front of the ash-clogged fireplace and wondered what and who this thing she called her husband was? Her past was so fuzzy. Had he ever been a man? Or was it a worm that had always stood beside her?

She crept up the stairs.

There she saw their dirty bathroom, their filthy bedroom, the closet full of piles of rubbish. Everything was the same, but corrupted. Spoiled. Everything, that is, except the spare room across the hall. The same one Tabitha had attempted to repaint a hundred times before. That imperfect room.

The door to it was closed. Tabitha went to open it, but was greeted instead by the sound of barking metal. She looked down and saw a chain wrapped around the doorknob several times and held in place by a thick padlock. She jerked the door again, to make sure it was as locked as it seemed. Sure enough, it didn't budge.

"What is this?" she asked The Worm Man who had slid up next to her. "Why is this room locked? Why can't I get in here?"

He ignored her question and instead motioned for her to follow.

"This is my house, right?" she said, standing firm. "Doesn't it belong to me? I need to look in there. This was my room, I was decorating it when it…all fell apart. I need to see it. I need to see what it looks like now. Is it complete?"

He pulsated, using his thick body to get in between her and the sealed room, and egged her forward. Chagrined and confused, the conviction in her voice simply melted away, without protest, as she left the door and followed the worm back down the stairs.

Together they passed through the soiled living room, through the equally tainted hall, the besmirched kitchen, and went out into the backyard.

And there, under the forever night of this black cave, and the fake crystal moon that oozed pallid light, and wind that was not wind, behind the house that was an echo of the house she was forced to leave behind, the yard was still intact. It was untouched by a shovel. Undug by a rake. There was no hole in it. And next to it, no spleenfruit tree grew.

It was a normal yard. Just like every other yard in this neighborhood.

In an instant, she forgot about the locked room upstairs. She turned to The Worm Man and smiled as joyful tears rolled out of her eyes.

She couldn't remember the last time she felt this happy.

18

The dress she wore had pictures of sunflowers printed all over it, yellow petals and skinny green stems against the cerulean fabric that hugged her bosoms and tapered out at her hips. She found it in the bedroom, a welcome change of clothing from the blood-caked outfit she had been wearing since she pulled herself out of the grisly ocean all those...hours...days...months...years...ago?

She had tried cleaning the house, for a while at least, but it never got any better. She'd sweep up a pile of dust and turn around to find a new layer covering the floor again. She'd drag the trash can out to the curb, but a garbage truck never came by to pick it up. She'd scrub the windows and it would only smear the filth across it in brown arches, like a colorless rainbow plastered against the glass. The water that came out of the sink was black. If she were to switch on the TV, every station would be filled with gray static.

But it was safe and it was easy. No one expected anything of her. No one bothered her.

And so she was happy.

I mean, this was what happiness felt like, right?

Don't think about that, Tabitha...

I mean...what even *is* happiness anyway?

Tabitha, are you listening to me...

What's in the spare room?

Why is it locked?

Her bed was a mound of dirt with a tarp thrown over top of it. The Worm Man would sleep under the tarp and she would sleep on top.

And then it was Saturday. And the only reason she was aware it had become Saturday was because the doorbell rang and when she opened it, Brad and Jennifer Flatly were standing there.

"Hey-ho, neighborinos!" said Brad. "You guys ready to barbeque or what!"

Brad Flatly had no eyes.

They had been eaten out of his skull and replaced by black voids. In the hollowed-out sockets a few small worms still dangled, swinging like miniature pendulums each time Brad moved his head. The same with Jennifer, this eyeless woman standing next to her groom, her skin emaciated and pruned, like it had been sucked dry of all its juices. Starved tendons wrapped around their birdlike bones, held in place by an ashen layer of latex-thin skin. They were covered in welts and pulsating sores, leaking what little fluid had been left to pump through their veins. A pink trail of it dripped from Jennifer's nose.

"Pardon me," she said, using the back of her hand to wipe it up. "It's just my brains. They've been liquefied, ya know. Eaten and digested by all the parasites living in my head. Turned into goop."

They sat in lawn chairs on the patio in the Tabitha's backyard. Big empty smiles on their gruesome faces, teeth already having been pushed out of their inky gums. They seemed as lively and enthusiastic as ever though, despite their physical appearances.

Tabitha sat across from the couple, shrunk up in her seat, trying not to get sick from having to look at them.

For his part, The Worm Man sat there too, complacent and quiet while the neighbors chatted away, reacting the way you'd expect a worm to react to such horrors, which is to say, not reacting at all.

Occasionally he'd shift in his seat, making a banana-like squish as he did so, but other than that, he remained aloof.

"You'd be surprised just how little use you have for your brain once it's mostly gone," Jennifer continued. "Until it started running out of my nose and down my face, I hardly even thought about it at all."

"Doesn't it…hurt?" Tabitha asked softly.

"Oh GOD yes!" Jennifer exclaimed.

"The pain is excruciating and unending," Brad calmly added. "But you just kinda get used to it. And after a while, it doesn't quite sting as much. Then, a little more time passes and you don't even notice it anymore. You just go about your day, just like every day, and any pain you felt before is now just a part of your existence. No more intrusive than a yawn. What more could you ask for, really?"

"Salad?" asked Jennifer, offering up a spoonful of wriggling grubs from the bowl they had brought over.

"No thanks, I'm not hungry," Tabitha said.

"Suit yourself," Jennifer replied, dumping the ladle of grubs down her own throat, not even attempting to chew. They climbed up into her head cavity and down into her esophagus, they wiggled out of her ears, they spilled out of the holes in her neck and chest, taking tiny bits and pieces of her flesh with them as they fell. Jennifer didn't even notice.

"Where are we?" Tabitha asked. "What is this place?"

"What do you mean?" said Jennifer. "We're in your backyard."

"I know that," said Tabitha. "But *where* is my backyard? What city is this? How is any of this possible?"

"Oh boy, that's a loaded question. You wanna take this one, Brad?" Jennifer asked.

"I sure can!" her husband cheerfully replied, sliding up in his chair and placing a skeletal hand on Tabitha's knee. He paused for a beat before continuing. "We're on the other side."

"The other side?" she said.

"*As above, so below, as within, so without, as the universe, so the soul…*" he said.

"What?"

"I didn't come up with that quote, mind you," he said. "Actually, I found it on the internet, on this website that aggregates famous quotes that you can browse through. Pretty rad saying though, right? And appropriate."

"Am I dead?" Tabitha said.

"What? No. Not even close," he snickered.

"Are you dead?"

"Do I look dead?"

"Um…yes."

"Alright well granted I *look* dead, but I'm certainly not acting dead, and that's because I'm NOT. Dead things don't have conversations. They don't go on moving around and talking and smiling and eating and having backyard barbeques like this. Don't matter how many bugs they got filling 'em up, feasting on 'em: dead is dead."

"If we were dead—if *you* were dead—there wouldn't be any coming back," Jennifer chimed in. "There's no such thing as Heaven, not that that should come as any of a surprise. Mythology might help keep the world glued together upstairs, but you're not gonna find any real magic down here. Once the lights go out, there's only darkness left."

Tabitha reacted to this as if she had just tasted something bitter.

"There were all these bodies…lining the shore, ground up like sand, or sewn up into the landscape like a human blanket…and this…giant worm monster…"

"Tabitha, he's right next to you!" Jennifer said out of the side of her mouth, motioning slyly to The Worm Man.

"No, not him," she said. "He's my…"

"…husband?" Brad finished her sentence for her.

Her forehead wrinkled up and her nostrils flared out and she exhaled dramatically. It seemed like that was what she was supposed to say, but still, it didn't sit well with her.

"….my husband," she said it out loud herself.

Nah, it definitely didn't sit well.

The Worm Man continued to say nothing.

"No, she's talking about the BIG ONE," Jennifer said. "The one outside the city limits. The *thing* in the ocean of blood."

"Oh THAT worm monster!" Brad exclaimed. "You're gonna have to be more specific going forward, darling. There's a lot of different types of worms. But to answer your question, that's the first trial that anyone who makes it down here has to face. And as you saw, the vast majority of people don't quite escape it. They end up ripped apart and vomited back onto the shore. More often than not, that meeting is of the terminal variety."

"And then there's the second trial," said Jennifer. "Getting past the gate itself. Getting into the city limits. As you can see by the distinct lack of other human beings around, not too many figure out how to open it. They just stand there like idiots, until they melt into the ground. Then they remain there, forever immobilized, forced to watch others step up to the gate and prosper or perish, but unable to intercede. Some people might argue that that's a fate worse than death."

"But how did I get it open?" asked Tabitha. "The gate? I don't remember how I got it open…"

"That's a good question," said Jennifer. "I suspect you had to confront some sorta uncomfortable truth and then, for better or worse, move on. That's kinda how things work down here. Emotional catharsis is the only currency that seems to matter in these parts. Unfortunately, most people are impoverished in that regard, an' they don't even realize it until it's way too late. They don't get anywhere. They're hopeless."

"So is there a third trial?" said Tabitha after a slight pause.

"A what?"

"A third trial?" Tabitha repeated herself. "After this? Some other place I need to go, or some other thing I need to do? Is this…the end?"

"How should we know?" said Jennifer. "We made it. We're here, back home, on Sycamore Lane. And that's all that matters. Right, honey?"

"Right, Jen," he said.

"Honestly, what more could we possibly ask for?"

"And Jen and I are just tickled pink that you're here too," Brad added. "We would've never guessed it, but as sure as I breathe, here you are."

"I'm so confused," said Tabitha, running her fingers through her greasy hair.

"This is really cute," Jennifer said, giving her husband a sheepish smile. "It's like she thinks she's the only person to ever fall down a hole before."

"Tabitha, you've looked in a mirror before, right?" Brad said.

"Huh?"

"A mirror. Like in the bathroom? Or on the inside door of an armoire?"

"Yes, I've looked in a mirror."

"Thing about mirrors is, they only show you things that are there, right? That's how they work. So that reflection you're getting is the world that surrounds you. The only thing you're gonna find in that mirror is yourself, flipped around backwards, and all the things behind you that you normally wouldn't be able to see when you're just facing forward."

"He's speaking in metaphors, sweetie," Jennifer interjected.

"Now, some people can't handle that; the flipside of where they're supposed to be facing," he continued. "And all that shit they left lying in the wake behind them, all that shit they were too afraid to confront, it tends to grow bigger and meaner in the darkness. It grows until it's out of their control. And when there's no place else left to go, and they're forced to look upon the mess they've created head-on, they let it tear 'em up. Tear 'em into pieces, so to speak. All those fragments of people you seen on the beach, those are the ones who let the mirror win, who let things in the darkness destroy them…"

"But not you," Jennifer said to Tabitha. "You made it back home."

"Is this my home?" she mumbled.

"This is a journey into yourself," said Brad. "Even if our love for each other, or lack thereof, was uninspired, it was good enough. We still liked our stupid little house and our stupid little neighborhood. We even liked you guys and the BBQs we'd have on Saturday nights. That's why we came over. We're having fun! We can have fun again, if we pretend. Isn't this fun?"

Tabitha was silent for a moment. Letting all this information sink in. And when she turned back to her gaunt and cadaverous neighbors, she asked them, very simply:

"So what happens next?"

The Flatlys exchanged a quick glance.

"What are you talking about?" said Brad. "Nothing. This is it."

19

Now, two important things are about to happen over the next few chapters that will alter the course of the rest of this book – hopefully in ways that you as a reader will find both unpredictable, and illuminating – because despite what Brad Flatly just said to Tabitha Moss, this certainly wasn't "it."

The first important thing that is going to happen is that Tabitha is going to swallow a seed, just like Harrison did, all-those-many pages ago. It's going to come full circle like that! And this will, of course, be the impetus for the second important thing that is going to happen, which is that Tabitha is going to break into the locked "spare room" upstairs.

Once she does that (and once we resolve that horrifying little scene with Harrison and The Worm Woman in the nightclub) we'll be ready to barrel, full-steam, into this novel's third act.

Imagine that! The third act! Already! How did we get here so fast? Wow, it really went quick!

But let's not get ahead of ourselves:

We're still in the backyard, at this barbeque, Brad and Jennifer Flatly sitting opposite Tabitha and The Worm Man. The steam rising from the cricket patties on the grill (oh yeah, they eat cricketburgers down here, YUM!) mimics the steam rising from the volcano violently juxtaposed next to the center of downtown. It gurgled and burped, as volcanos tend to do, but Tabitha and her company couldn't hear that from their current location, because Brad, once again, started talking.

"Hey, what's with the long face, neighbor?" he said. "Isn't this what you wanted? A return to normalcy?"

"I...don't know what I want anymore..."

"Oh lordy," he chuckled to his wife. "I think she might be having an existential crisis or something."

"It certainly seems that way," said Jennifer. "Course, it's a little late for that."

"Normalcy..." Tabitha echoed. "Is *that* what I'm after?"

"Isn't it?"

"I remember, when we first moved in here, when the moving truck rumbled up past all those green trees, the pastel houses cloistered up on this dead end street, it all seemed so...plain. Boring. We had just moved out of the city. We looked at you guys and we *mocked* you. We didn't want to live a life of complacency. That wasn't why we got together, fell in love. We went to bed that night promising each other we'd never let the routine remold us."

"Wait, you mocked us?" an offended Jennifer Flatly said as bugs spewed forth from her excavated eyeholes. "I don't get it. What's wrong with us?"

"Nothing," said Tabitha. "Nothing is wrong with you. That was the point. You guys just seemed so *normal*. And the love I shared with this guy, What's-His-Name, it felt so different. I didn't want it to be normal."

"What's-His-Name?" Jennifer repeated.

"You guys remember his name? You guys remember him, don't you?"

"He wasn't this worm fellow that you're with?" said Brad, motioning to the handsome worm still seated next to them.

"It could be because insects ate most of my brains," Jennifer nodded. "But as far as I can recall, I'm pretty certain you've always lived here with this worm man. Your husband."

"No," Tabitha said, shaking her head. "No, that's not right. He wasn't always a worm. He was a man, once." She sighed and continued. "I was so lost. Lonely. At the end of my rope. I couldn't see anything beyond the day, the day that I met him. I was in that Home Depot, I was ready to..."

She paused. Took a deep breath.

"And then…all of a sudden…there was this guy. He wasn't there yesterday, and then, all of a sudden, today he was. Our paths aligned. And that was it. We were entwined from there on out. It was an accident, this whole thing was an accident. Falling in love is an accident. It just happens. Happened – I should say. Past tense. Because it *had* happened. We *had* fallen into love. And once we got there, it was like, what else? We took the same steps we saw people take before us. A wedding. A home. A job. We weren't special, were we? Our love wasn't special. We were just like everyone else. So we grew comfortable, with our lives, with each other, with everything…

"I wonder, is comfort the enemy of passion? Should people in love strive to stay uncomfortable? Is that the trick? Should we acknowledge how tenuous and fleeting our grasp on the future is? Should we set our houses on fire? Should we even have houses at all? And if we don't have houses, then where do we sleep? And if we can't sleep, then when do we dream? And if we're not dreaming, then where else do we have left to go…?"

And then, right there, as if jolted by an electric shock, she understood the reason that Harrison felt compelled to dig that hole.

"Harrison." Tabitha whispered to herself. "That is his name. His name is Harrison."

An escape hatch. A way out. Something to hope for. He started digging the hole to try and save them, not to bury them in. She could see it now, as plain as the words of this paragraph. The way up was down, the way out was in. *As above, so below…*

She threw herself out of the chair and onto the lawn. On her hands and knees she crawled across the yard, blades of wispy dead grass scratching her skin, giving way slightly under the weight of her body. The neighbors watched silently. So did The Worm Man. She slithered her way to the center of the yard, and found the spot where her husband had first began to dig. She herself was not a worm, but she moved with the dexterity of one as she stuck her hands into the soil and pulled a couple of large scoops out.

"The hole is still here!" she shouted.

"A hole can be anywhere," Brad tried to rationalize with her. "All you have to do is dig. But it doesn't have to *mean* anything."

She ignored him as she burrowed down, excavating just a few

inches of dirt before coming across something that was buried in there. She pushed against it. It was firm and rubbery, like a car tire, but smaller. She brushed the earth from the top of it and stood up, wrapping her fingers around its sides. She pulled. She pulled with all her might. And then, it popped out of the ground and Tabitha fell backwards, landing on her butt.

In her lap was a spleenfruit.

Purple and muscular, throbbing like it had its own heartbeat.

"I hated that tree," she said. "It grew in our backyard, so creepy. Like a big ol' hand trying to punch the sky. But here it is, nascent, just a shitty little fruit, buried under the ground and forgotten. It hadn't even begun to sprout yet. Even the biggest trees start out as the smallest seeds."

She squeezed it. The rind turned from deep purple to lavender as it stressed against its own seams before rupturing open. White, ovular seeds squirted out in an efflux of clear fluid. It ejected itself all over Tabitha's sunflower dress, the smell of rancid meat wafting up from the goop. In another state of mind, Tabitha might've gagged, dry-heaved, turned her head and ran as fast and as far as she could from this vile situation. But here, in this moment, she didn't even wince. Instead, she plucked a singular seed out of the seminal slop. Held it up. It glistened and quivered in her trembling hands.

And then she put it in her mouth and swallowed it.

"Disgusting," Jennifer Flatly remarked as her brains leaked out of her nose and ears and pieces of her scalp fell off in wet clumps and bugs climbed in and out of the gory, open wounds covering her pallid and dehydrated flesh.

20

So now we skip ahead a few hours.

Brad and Jennifer Flatly had already said their goodbyes, shambled their ghastly corpses back to the tomb of their own home.

"Hey Tabitha," Brad said right before he left. "I'm not quite sure what you're searching for, or what the point of any of this really is, but I hope you figure it all out."

And that was the last we were going to hear from The Flatlys, at least for the rest of this book.

So long and thanks for all the exposition, you two!

And then it was later that night. Past midnight. Or rather, it *would've* been past midnight if this were the kind of place that could discriminate between day and night. But as it were – as it always was down here – this city, and by extension, this odd version of Sycamore Lane, continued to be dark and sticky and underground.

Tabitha suddenly woke up from a deep slumber.

She could hear The Worm Man, stirring slightly underneath the tarp of their bed, but he didn't even poke his head out as she stood up and made her way out of the room, down the hallway, down the stairs, out into the backyard.

Reality felt as firm as a wet piece of silk. Her thoughts were as concrete as the air itself.

Here she stood, in her nightgown, guts twisting and turning inside her stomach as the spleenfruit seed sprouted and took hold; the roots plucked her veins like a guitar and strung up her sinews like they had been sent to the gallows, and were this seed able to talk to her like a child talks into a tin can telephone, she would've heard it repeating the same message, over and over and over again:

To the shed. Go to the shed.

So she did.

Here, she found the collection of tools her husband had left, stored in the cramped shed's dustiest corners. Screwdrivers and pliers and power drills and saws; either hanging on the walls or stashed away in boxes or shelves.

"Nothing is broken," she had said to Harrison on the day he bought all that useless hardware. "Aren't you going to feel stupid when you realize you spent all this money on, say, that chop saw right there, only to never use it?"

To which he simply replied: "Darling, you never know what tool you're gonna need until the moment you need it."

She reached out and picked up an axe.

She cut back across the yard, dragging the axe through the yellow grass behind her. It was heavier than she would've guessed.

Back up the stairs.

In the hallway. In front of the spare room.

She tried the handle one last time. Jiggled and jerked it. Locked as it ever was.

And then she took the axe and slammed it into the door.

Hey, remember that scene in *The Shining* when Jack Torrance is swinging that axe at the bathroom door, smashing it up into little pieces, and then he pokes his head through and says "Here's Johnny!" as his terrified family screams and cries. THIS MOMENT WAS JUST LIKE THAT! Except there was no terrified family on the other side of that door. The terrified person was the one wielding the axe. It felt like fireworks inside her head, a cannonade, a firestorm exploding across synapses.

Tears rolled down her cheeks and her spine felt like it was twisted up with vines, the spleenfruit growing inside of her, clawing apart her veins. Her arms burned with every strike. She screamed. Primal. It was coming out of her like lava from the lips of a volcano. Oh god, these walls, these walls, these suffocating walls. This isn't her house. Whose house is this? Where the fuck was she?!?

And the door splintered apart. It fell in jagged wooden pieces. And she stepped through it.

Here is what the spare room looked like:

There was a throw rug in the center of the floor, pastel and soft against her bare feet. It was clean, freshly vacuumed, swept, and sterilized. A crib was pushed into the far corner, the wood on the bars polished and new, like it had just been assembled.

From the windows, light spilled in. Daylight. Summer light. Like it was a June afternoon outside.

Tabitha scarcely had time to contemplate the logistical impossibility of this; how the sun might be shining in this one room only, from a sky which has no sun, when she saw the walls.

The color.

After spending years upon years, buckets upon buckets, coats upon coats, she had needlessly and endlessly TOILED for this stupid room. And now here it was, without any of her help, needing to be repainted no more. Complete.

It was the perfect color.

Language completely failed her. She was speechless. In awe.

It was not a simple combination of *THIS MUCH* red and *THAT MUCH* blue, because that would just make a new shade of purple, and purple was just fucking purple, after all. You know what purple looks like. Purple can be *explained.*

No no no, language failed this color because it contradicted the eye to even see it. It was a color, and yet, it *wasn't* – matte yet bright, in defiance of rainbows. We could call it *urtawrk* or *boodert* or *mallorgn* or whatever the hell made-up word we wanted, it didn't matter, because it was all nonsense at this point anyway. How would YOU even begin to describe what something called *mallorgn* looks like, anyway?

The axe slipped from her hand and she fell to her knees. Palms up. Eyes moist. What felt like madness roaring through in her head before now shifted into...who knows what! There were too many damn emotions to be able to name them all, if they even had names to begin with. Just like the color on the walls of this room, her feelings were a blur heretofore unknowable.

And then:

The mobile above the crib spun. All by itself. IT WAS SO SPOOKY, JUST LIKE IN A HORROR MOVIE! Not *The Shining*, this time. A different horror movie.

The mobile was made up of three plastic beetles, clear fishing line affixed to a small loop on their backs, wings out like they were in the midst of flight. They moved in a slow, tight circle as creepy *ting-ting* lullaby music played.

Tabitha dried her eyes, sniffled up her snot, got a grip on herself, looked towards the revolving mobile like it were the clock ticking down on the side of a time bomb. She stood up. Toes back on the carpet, pointed towards the crib. And the closer she stepped in that direction, the darker it got outside. The sun, or whatever it was, disappeared like someone had lowered the temperature on a knob. Grayness took its place. Decay crept in. It overcame those perfectly painted walls.

The room got cold.

The sound that the mobile made was so fucking evil, holy shit!

She placed her hands on the edge of the crib, and slowly peeked inside.

And there was nothing there.

She let out a sigh of relief. She expected something terrifying. Or at least something really gross. An alien bug baby, or *something*. But nope.

She turned to leave to room. And that's when The Worm Man attacked her.

21

All at once, he was on top of her. Wrapping his slender body around her like a bungee cord.

He pulled himself taut and the wind was forced out of her lungs.

He twisted like a pretzel around her ankles. She tried to run but he tripped her up. She fell. As soft as the rug had appeared to be before, there was still wood underneath it, and that wood was hard, and when she landed on it, cheek first, it HURT, like: *Thud!* and then there was a red line crisscrossing her face where the skin had split, and The Worm Man was wrapping himself around her tighter, and the blood in her chest was squeezed up to her head, squirting out of the wound like melted ice cream. It puddled underneath her and clotted in her hair. She couldn't move.

All of this had happened so quickly that she didn't even have the chance to scream until The Worm Man was already knotted up around all of her limbs and his pointy, expressionless face was hovering menacingly just a few inches above hers.

"Help!" she cried out as loud as she could, which wasn't very loud at all. Certainly not loud enough for anyone to do anything about it. The plea that escaped her lips was no more a scream than a float with a flat tire was a parade.

"Someone, please help!"

* * *

Tabitha was lying powerless on the floor of the room she had painted and repainted a thousand times before, the monster on top of her in complete control, and she was crying for help like someone would actually come swoop in and save her. Like the word 'help' meant anything down here, under the ground. Like help was even an option anymore. No, you're not going to see the Flatlys come bursting through the door, their empty bones jangling across the room as they pulled the assailing Worm Man off her in the nick of time; then the three of them absconding away, down the road, all safe and sound forevermore. And you're certainly not going to see Harrison Moss come suddenly smashing through the window pane, landing in front of her in a hurricane of shattered glass, two bandoliers of ammo strapped across his somehow now-muscular chest, finger on the trigger of a semiautomatic rifle, unloading a volley of bullets into this aggravated annelid like he was Arnold Schwarzenagaggennnnnagreazzenagerer taking down the bad guys at the climax of *Commando*.

Neither of those things were going to happen. Instead we have this:

The worm forced her legs open wide and pressed his body against the skin of her thighs.

Her wide eyes rolled over to the crib, then back to him.

"Why?" she eked.

Everything had gone blurry.

He was secreting something. Oozy and thick and white, covering his rigid flesh. It was coming out of his skin in pearly globs. It was worm cum. He was cumming all over the place, lubricating them both. It smelled foul, and Tabitha got sick. Vomit and blood, pouring out of her face, swirling together, sloshing around underneath them, swirled up like the colors in a peppermint candy.

He held her down.

Her dress slipped past her thighs and up to her waist.

Her chest heaved in and out. Hyperventilating. She was suffocating in her own body.

The Worm Man took his lower end and shoved it between her legs.

Tabitha yelped and futilely thrashed.

* * *

Here were The Worm Man's ultimate intentions:

He was going to enter her. He was going to climb inside of her skin. He was going to make her pregnant with him. He was going to infest her, live inside her, wear her like a suit, become her. And then, when he was done, he would give birth back to himself. He was going to consume her, in her totality, gnawing away from the inside out. He was going to eat her past, present, and future, give it back to the dirt because, to a worm, a human body isn't worth more than the mud it had been created from.

He was going to fuck her up.

He was going to fuck her.

But he couldn't!

And not for lack of will. And he certainly tried.

No, he couldn't fuck her up because there was nothing there for him to fuck.

There was nothing between her legs but a flat patch of skin. Like the inner part of an elbow. She was a Barbie doll beneath her skirt. She had no vagina. She had nothing at all.

She had known this, of course, as did you, the reader, because it had been discussed before. She had willfully let her genitals disappear, a physical manifestation of her inner turmoil. Any trace of passion she had held on to had been stolen away by apathy years before. She had let that apathy in. Let it metastasize. Let it take over. She had let it claim her relationship. Claim her womanhood. Claim her life.

And it dawned on Tabitha, right then as The Worm Man's lower half forced itself into the space between her hips, pressing against the flat spot, searching in vain for the opening he expected to be there, that her body was not his to take or exploit. He would not be able to assert himself over her, if she didn't let him. For he possessed no real power; he was just a parasite, after all, and she was a human being. She had chosen this life. She had willed her pussy away. She had brought herself here, to this fake house constructed as a poor facsimile to the real thing. And if she wanted to leave, all she had to do was get up and go.

The Worm Man's head cocked to the side.

Do you think that will stop us? You think we can't find another way into your skin? You are nothing but a nest, Tabitha. An incubator that thinks its life means something more. You are nothing but me-e-e-e-at.

Those words materialized in her head, intruded in from the ether, pushing out all her other thoughts. She grit her teeth and exhaled loudly, searching for that voice in her brain she recognized as her own.

"Even if I can't stop you..." Tabitha Moss grunted aloud to the creature on top of her as she reached over and grabbed the handle of the axe in her right hand, "...I can certainly try!"

She swung the weapon into The Worm Man's back.

He unraveled immediately, untangling himself from her, reeling back, his injured body like a bullwhip, thrashing around. Tabitha dodged his wild swings as he tried to escape, slithering on his belly towards the exit. But Tabitha, quickly back on her feet, determinedly walked over to the creature. She stepped on his tail and pulled the axe out of his back. He writhed in pain. The fluid he had been secreting earlier had turned from white to pink. He turned around to face her. Helpless. Pleading.

"Ashes to ashes and dust to dust, motherfucka!" she said – a line cheesy enough to be spoken by Arnold Schwarzenagaggennnnnagreazzenagerer himself – as she swung down with all her might, chopping The Worm Man completely in half.

His two halves wiggled. Bled. Then stopped wiggling.

She took off, down the stairs and out the front door. She ran down the street, away from the cul-de-sac.

In the distance, the volcano softly rumbled.

22

On the floor of a warehouse rave Harrison Moss was lying too, held
to the ground, at the mercy of this seductive and vicious Worm
Woman on top of him.

He was not as strong as his wife. That should've been established
long ago. He had let the madness in early. It could be argued that
he was the one who pulled her into this madness with him, and that
Tabitha was and remains an innocent bystander, merely trying to
cope with the desperate whims of an obsessive and unhinged man.
But to argue that would be selling her short as a character, depriving
her of an arc in which she can learn and grow as a person, as surely
Harrison is about to do, in the most bizarre and disgusting way.

(NOTE: Interpretations as to the intent of the author in regards
to some of the more metaphorical aspects of this story may vary
depending on your personal experience and biases. The point remains
that whereas Tabitha was able to fend her assailant off and escape,
Harrison hadn't had this revelation until it was too late.)

So here's what happened:

The Worm Woman entered his mouth, forcing her way down
his throat. She filled him up like the spleenfruit had. He could feel
her sticky figure as it pushed its way further and further into him.
Into his stomach. His bowels. The curves of her body that he once

thought were sexy now pushed against the underside of his skin like the water in a balloon that was begging to burst. He was a blood balloon that was going to explode.

She was eating up his insides.

If you're unaware of the role that worms play, ecologically-speaking, allow me to elaborate. I know you're not supposed to go off on too many tangents, especially while the action is rising (such as now, as The Worm Woman burrows through our protagonist's guts) but it's important to the story. Just trust me, okay?

Worms eat decaying organic matter; leaves and manure and other detritus. They eat up and digest the dirt, which in turn helps to aerate it, improving its fertility. Healthy soil is a necessary part of any sustainable ecological system.

Of course, Harrison had lungs which he could breathe from and he didn't need to be aerated. Still, The Worm Woman ate. His internal organs passed through her as it would pass through all worms, maw to belly and beyond, until it is eventually excreted out the other end. This substance was called vermicompost – or, more colloquially – worm shit. Worms eat old soil and shit out nutrient-rich soil in its place. This was the kind of soil that aided plant growth. The kind of soil, let's say, in which the seed of a spleenfruit tree might finally find the kind of purchase it needed to vibrantly, terrifyingly grow.

The Worm Woman was eating Harrison up from the inside out and filling his body with her shit. And the spleenfruit seed he had swallowed ALLLLLLLLLLLLLL the way back at the beginning of this book, the spleenfruit seed that had squeezed his veins and seized his brains, it grew, rapidly. Way more rapidly than before. Finding all the nourishment it could possibly need in the now-abundant mulch that his innards had become, the spleenfruit bore its roots deep into his flesh.

She travelled all the way through him, evacuating herself out of his body in the same way the dirt was evacuating hers: the bottom. She came out of his asshole, covered in shit and slime, filth and blood. Harrison convulsed on the dancefloor while The Worm Woman smugly coiled above him.

Brown foam poured out of his mouth, spilling down his cheeks. His eyes wide. Gagging.

And then came the leaves.

They sprouted on the tip of his tongue and sprung from every cut on his body. A bouquet. A goddamn forest coming out of him. He had been fertilized.

"Wha – what did you do?" he said as he stood up.

A lungful of mulch spilled out of his face every time he opened his mouth. He could feel it like mucous inside his body. The vegetation proliferating faster than he could possibly expunge it. And when he spoke, it pushed its way past his lips and garbled up his words so that he sounded like he was choking on marbles.

The Worm Woman was smiling. Well, not *literally* smiling, but the worm equivalent to smiling, which to the untrained eye looked like nothing. She couldn't smile, her physiology wasn't capable of it, but Harrison could sense it. He knew she was smiling, just like he knew that this is what she would be saying if she had a voice:

You are my house. You are my dirt. You are my everything, Harrison Moss. You are my planet.

Those were the words that formed delicately inside his head.

"What are you talking about?!" he shouted. "What does that MEAN?!!"

Hmmm. That was a little vague, wasn't it? Should I rewrite that line? Who would even say something that? Like, what *does* it mean?

"See, even the narrator is mocking you!" he said to The Worm Woman, pointing to the paragraph just before this one.

She remained unfazed as his skin pulsated out in bubbles like his insides were boiling. It hurt.

"Why are you all doing this to me?" he shouted to the entire room, to all the other insects watching from the balconies and the building's wings. "What is the point of trying to get to the bottom of things when the answers we uncover are even more convoluted than the questions we ask? Why did you whisper in my head?"

Better question is: why did you swallow the seed in the first place?

"I DON'T KNOW!" he said. More leaves shot out of his mouth. They were growing out of his ears and nose. From all around the edges of his eyelids, wispy roots hung like corn silk; potato roots sprouted across his face like acne. "I don't know why I swallowed it, okay? I don't know what's wrong with me. I don't know why I don't know how to be happy." He took a laborious and exasperated breath. "I tried to fight it, to deny the apathy access to the footholds it had slowly carved into my life, but I gave up. That's how it wins. We eventually get tired of trying to stop it. Because there is no stopping it. I ate the seed because, what else was I going to do? And then I pulled my wife down here with me and I don't know if she was ready for that, but I was desperate. I pulled her into this hole and now I'm turning into a fucking plant and she's gone."

He looked at The Worm Woman. If he could've cried, he would've, but the roots inside his body drank up all his tears before he could squelch them out.

"It's too late to stop this, isn't it?"

The Worm Woman didn't respond. Didn't move. She just stood there, motionless, her body shaped like a crooked S. The shadows from the darkest parts of the club crept up to meet her, to take her away.

"Wait, where are you going?" he said.

There was panic in his voice. He knew that once she left, she was never coming back again. This was the wicked way of love; it cut through your life without remorse, sometimes flourishing, sometimes ravishing. Harrison was the dirt in which these buds would bloom, and in the end, buried. His body was her vessel, and now she was leaving. Her work here was done.

His shoes had broken open as roots pushed themselves out of the ends of his toes and made their way for the ground below. He had to keep moving his legs, up and down, to keep from getting stuck.

"You can't just leave me here in this…place. I'm a man, not a plant. You can't just rip apart my insides and then disappear. That's not fair. That's not how it should work."

She said nothing. Like the apparition she appeared to be the first time he saw her, the thought-form on the edge of perception that all memories take, she once again fell into the shadows.

He had no one to blame but himself, of course. He had followed this road to its deadest of ends. Just like the house in the cul-de-sac on Sycamore Lane; he had nowhere left to go.

He looked up at The Worm Woman. She was almost gone completely. Faded away forever. There was only one thing left he could possibly do to stop her. He took a breath, his lungs full of flowers, and he charged, screaming, into the darkness.

He leapt onto her. She tumbled backwards, letting out a shocked hiss. When her maw opened, he saw teeth, sharp like a shark's. He pulled her out of the shadows and threw her back onto the dancefloor.

"I don't know what you are, or what you're supposed to be, but I won't let you go that easily," he screamed.

Although the club had gone eerily silent, the colored lights and strobes still flashed, adding a circus-like quality to the melee. The DJ, a slug named MC Saltshaker (why not?) sensed this and played some circus-like music to accompany the scene.

Can you see this in your head? It was like a fucking circus. And I know circuses are supposed to be fun, but...

He was straddling her, The Worm Woman thrashing around under him, trying to free herself to no avail. For the first time in a long time, he had the upper hand. Heh, get it? The upper *hand*. And he didn't even have *hands*. Irony! See, it IS kinda fun, right?

He shoved his shovel hand down as hard as he could, swinging it with the precision of a guillotine, striking her right in the center of her torso.

The edges of the shovel had been whet from all the miles of digging he had done, now as sheened and sharp as a Bowie blade, and it sliced right through her. Like she was nothing more than Jell-O.

The force of his blow drove the trowel through her entire body. Chopped her in two. It came out of her back in an explosion of white worm guts and embedded itself into the concrete floor, wedging itself tighter than the sword Excalibur.

Her two halves wiggled around, violent and desperate, before finally throwing Harrison off her and, in the process, ripping the shovel hand from his body. It didn't want to come off, not easily, after being fused to his arm bones. But the force was such that it came off anyway, in a geyser of hot blood and brown foliage, his wrist torn open.

But he didn't remain handless for long.

The plant inside him rushed for the opening, replacing his missing extremity. Long, bark-covered branches crawled out of the wound. Five branches, one for each finger. They hung, a dozen inches each, twisty digits that were barely functional. He could flex his muscle and get them to twitch, but that was about it. He wasn't going to be playing a piano or painting the Sistine Chapel with these fingers. He wasn't going to be doing much of anything, except running for the exit to the club, running as fast as his tree trunk legs could carry him, out into the world.

"If at every instant we may perish,
so that at every instant we may be saved."
—Jules Verne, *Journey to the Center of the Earth*

PART THREE
BETWEEN

23

Here we are now on the outskirts of this Nowhere City.

Even after all we've been through, we're still wandering. Still lost.

Here are the thoughts that pass through our head, as we walk alone down these endless streets:

Did we really think that burying all of our problems was going to make them disappear?

How adorably naïve we were! Clearly, that was not the case. That is never the case.

Did we think that this journey we were forced into was going to reveal something meaningful about humanity? Or at the very least, reveal to us something meaningful about ourselves?

Hahaha! Give me a break! That's not how this works. This is fiction. A story. It's all fake. He dug a hole in his backyard and ended up burying himself? C'mon, even that metaphor is trite. There's no subtly to it. It's overwrought and obvious. It's pulp. It's hack. This whole thing is the work of a hack.

I mean, look at it. Look at these stupid words. Can you people not put it together? I'm not even trying to hide it anymore. I've done away with any pretense of authorial detachment and just switched over into first-person perspective. This book is my hole! THIS BOOK IS ALL ABOUT ME!

I once heard an author I really respect talking about how it's the *responsibility* of the writer to not waste their reader's time. How, in writing as a trade, we should be mindful of our audience and the fact that they've decided to invest time in our art. As such, the people who picked up this book didn't do so to hear *my* story. Nobody cares about *my* story. They're reading this book to hear *their* story through the eyes of somebody else. You, the reader, are supposed to be the main character here. Not me, the creator.

But the thing I'm struggling with is this: how the hell am I supposed to tell YOUR story? Where would I even start? How could I possibly know if this story has been about you at all? I don't know you and when I try to think about who you may be, you appear to me as faint and allusive as The Worm Woman first appeared to Harrison. To me, you are an abstract notion. A giant blur. And in that blur, you could be ANY of the 8 billion other people on this planet, each one with their own hopes, their own struggles. There's no way I could possibly narrow THAT down into something you might find relatable. Because maybe you're not like me. Maybe we have nothing in common. Maybe you've got it all together. Maybe you've never once questioned any of your relationships. Or your job. Or your life. Or anything. Maybe you like your books to be light, fluffy reads. Maybe you picked this novel up because you were simply looking to be entertained. And that's totally fine by me! I don't have a problem with that! I like to be entertained too! But how am I supposed to know how to entertain you when you've never ONCE made a wrong turn and you're just so very happy, and here I am, the only sonofabitch in the entire universe who feels forced to accept responsibility like it was a goddamn noose around his neck?

It makes me wonder, how much neurosis can I cram into one book before anyone notices that I'm doing it? And now, look at this: I'm not trying to hide it anymore. I've fallen off the wagon completely. This isn't a story. This is a journal entry. This is terrible.

And, OH GOD, what is my wife going to say when she reads this manuscript? I hadn't even considered the fact that she's going to read this thing before it goes to print. Will she understand I'm merely trying to explore the darker side of relationships, and of normalcy, like we should all be so fucking happy that everything turned out okay, if we can even consider the life we've been living to be okay? Or will she take this personally? Will she scream at me? Beg me not to publish it? Worse, will she divorce me, or murder me in my sleep?

Will my editor even keep this self-indulgent, 4ᵗʰ wall-breaking diatribe in the final draft?

And speaking of final drafts, how the FUCK am I going to end this thing? I can see my word count in the document that I'm typing this up in. I can see it going up with every new sentence. I see the little mark on my calendar, indicating my approaching deadline. I know we've entered the third act; that we're quickly coming up on that ending, and that it's time to land this rickety-old-plane-of-a-novel on the runway. BUT HOW? Despite everything we've been through, and everything I've just said, I don't want to waste your time. I need to make all this bullshit PAY OFF without relying on one those tacked on *happily-ever-after* type endings, because the moments after that kind of ending are where this book began, and I don't want to leave you with a contrived and oversimplified moral like "love conquers all" or some other type of unctuous nonsense.

I want it to *FEEL* real.

And I want you to *FEEL* it too.

So to that end, no more of this meta-analysist stuff. It's distracting. Just the story, cut and dry, from here on out. Until we're done.

Under the ground:

Harrison wandered the city. His body had become more and more plant-like (and, adversely, less and less human) with each lugubrious step.

Mixed in with the leaves and foliage were a few odd fingers he had somehow begun to regenerate. Not a hand, exactly. Not even close. He wasn't going to be slapping anyone high-five anytime soon. But somewhere, amid the meat and vegetation beneath his skin, a mass of fingers had sprouted too, like carrots, and were using the surging rush of flora to push their way to the surface.

He didn't know when this transformation would end. If it would end. Heck, he didn't know if it was even a transformation at all. This could all be the symptoms of a new and strange fever, a temporary necrosis, a case of the sniffles, and it would soon pass. Perhaps this had all been a dream the whole time, or a hallucination, or the protracted and eternal flash that the terminal man may have pass before his eyes...

Of course, this was all wishful thinking on Harrison's part. What he wouldn't give for a simple fatal disease right about now! He knew that this was no mere hallucination, nor was it the symbolic projection of a fever dream. This shit was real, a fact no more evidenced than by the anguish of Tabitha Moss, who had been pulled down here to suffer too, independent of any other explanation that crossed Harrison's mind.

She was wandering the city just as Harrison did, but from the opposite end.

Both she and her husband had no specific destination they were headed. Everything was lost.

The insects infesting this city paid these two humans no more mind than a human would normally pay to a bug. If an acknowledgement was made, it was done with disinterest. Still, the closer they got to downtown, the more awake the city seemed to become. Worms hustled and bustled about. Some wore neckties, even though they had no necks, and some carried briefcases, even though they had no arms. Other worms ran shops and newsstands, serving up piles of warm, putrid trash the way a vendor might serve up a hotdog. Tourist worms took pictures of large, crumbling buildings on what appeared to be broken cameras. Near the alleyways there were worms who were clearly derelict, even though everything down here was covered with dirt, hustling for spare change. There was a worm analog for every type of person you could come across in the world topside.

The seed in Tabitha's stomach was doing things to her body too, just like it was doing things to her husband's, though not nearly as dramatic. Not yet.

For now, a malaise settled over her as she trudged through this nightmare world, alone. Such is malaise. And such is loneliness.

And as Harrison wandered, he came upon a store that he thought might help. It had helped him in the past, though the man he was then and the man he was now were as disparate as any two random souls you could compare.

Big and square and orange, this store was like a cartoon castle. It stood by itself in a massive parking lot. An island in a sea of tar.

It was a Home Depot, under the ground.

Harrison thought it was odd that Home Depot would choose to build a location here. But he supposed insects, like the creatures of the firma above, sometimes needed tools and supplies too.

Still, he wondered silently to himself, what use could a worm have for a hammer?

Harrison went inside the hardware store.

His plan was to purchase some pruning shears. He wanted to trim back some of these branches growing out of his skin, and try to keep himself mobile for as long as possible. It wasn't much of a plan, but it was better than nothing. Each step was getting harder. His feet were roots, ready to unfurl, trying to hold him in place.

He walked around the Home Depot, the aisles and rows like ramparts, like the walls of the dome that surrounded this city. It was as suffocating in the store as it was outside of it.

Worms pushed orange carts with wobbly wheels and shopped like it was just a normal Sunday and they needed to buy some plywood or a chandelier-style light fixture.

Harrison ignored them and they ignored him.

And when he happened across an aisle that on the endcap read ROPES, he paused.

Something about this all seemed so tragically familiar.

He went down the aisle and stopped in front of the rows of braided rope spools.

He thought about the first time he was here, all those years ago, on the day that Tabitha went from a faceless stranger to an inescapable part of his life. Everything was different from then on out.

"Do you know why I was here, on the day that we met?" a voice suddenly said. He turned his head to the side and there she was, Tabitha, standing next to him. He felt like he hadn't seen her in decades. Perhaps it had been that long. "Do you know why I was in this aisle in particular, standing right here, in front of the ropes?"

"I suspect it was the same reason I was," Harrison said. "You were planning on hanging yourself."

She sighed as if she had just been exonerated from some long-held confession. "Sometimes being a person is just so damn hard, ya know?"

"I thought your love was going to save me," he said. "I thought that was all there was. That's what these stories teach us, right? That if we're good people, then we fall in love and get a happy ending, because that's what good people deserve. We played by the rules and did everything right. And yet, here we are. It didn't change a thing. I was still the same as I always was on the inside."

"I know," she said. "I thought your love would save me too. I had nothing else."

"Were we ever in love?" he said. "Is such a thing even possible?"

"I've asked myself that countless times before."

"That day – the one when I swallowed the seed, cut off my hands, and started digging this bottomless hole – I was in the backyard, mowing the lawn. It was a day like the days that preceded it. Normal. As normal as it gets. And then…I don't know, Tabs. I felt it. I felt all the weight of that time piling up on top of me. I needed to do something about it. Something drastic. I needed to destroy it all. Or run away. Or rebuild it. Or *something*. I needed to *TRY*. How can I possibly get you to understand an emotion so imprecise and convoluted?"

She didn't reply. Not with big swooping proclamations of forgiveness, nor with ire or condemnation. She didn't drop the L-word, because that would cheapen this moment and reduce it to kitsch. Instead, she merely reached out and took ahold of the roots hanging off the end of his wrist into the palm of her hand.

"I understand," she softly said.

He looked up at her and in her eyes he could see it. Inside of her. Working its way through her veins.

"You ate a seed too?"

She nodded.

"What is it doing to you?" he asked.

"I don't know yet," she replied.

But it didn't really matter. His heart thundered in his chest, each palpitation sending a wave of euphoria through him. Her nostrils flared. Their bodies ran hot with desire and lust.

"You're here with me now?" he said.

"I am," she replied.

"So you know what we have to do then, yes?" he said.

She nodded again.

He didn't have to say anything else.

This is going to get gross.

Yes, this is going to get weird.

Because sometimes love is gross and weird.

And sometimes love is tender and soft.

And sometimes love is violent and terrifying.

And sometimes love is all these things, all at once. Especially when the seeds inside your body are flowering and flourishing and looking for a way to push themselves out. Sometimes love is not a thing that comes to you, like a gift from the gods, but something you have to discover, fight for, and earn. Sometimes it hibernates, deep within, and when it finally wakes up, it's ready to burn hotter than all the stars in the sky combined. For the first time in a long time, perhaps for the first time in their entire relationship, both Harrison and Tabitha let passion take over.

And right there, in the middle of this hardware store – surrounded by the tools and the bugs and the dirt and decay and the blood and the plants and everything else that makes this whole disgusting universe spin 'round – Harrison laid his wife down like the floor were as private as their honeymoon bed, and he climbed on top of his bride.

His skin split open, a fissure that ran from his bellybutton down past the crest of his perineum. Opening up, ever-so-slightly, like the parting of barn doors. It physically hurt him. You could see it on his face as he bit his lip and cried green tears. The pain caused him to inhale sharply, furrow his brow, wince. And out from this newly formed hole in his body wormed a singular root:

Thick and long.

Throbbing.

And phallic.

Tabitha was breathing hard too as his root pressed up against her groin. Her chest was pumping, up and down, in and out, nervous and excited and a little afraid, all at the same time. She too opened up, spreading wide, letting him in. And LORDY it was painful for her too! A gap between her legs appearing as if it were a peach pulled apart by invisible hands. She grimaced. Eyes watered, breath seized. A vaginal slit appeared, fleshy and raw and brand-spanking-new.

The two of them, without the means or the desire for so long, their genitals previously healed away like vestigial organs evolved out of two ravenous beasts, BUT NOW, re-evolved, exploding forth, unable to be suppressed or circumvented, human biology coming full circle in the most unchaste way. It was happening, in all its gooey glory. And, my god, it couldn't have possibly been any more poetic than the moment the two of them lovingly embraced and tenderly, earnestly, FINALLY had sex again.

Right there.

On the Home Depot floor.

24

Perhaps, in the world above, an act of indecency such as the act that Harrison and Tabitha had just committed on the floor might be cause for arrest. At the very least, they would've been kicked out of the store. But here, in the underground, amongst the creatures who thrive in the filth, nobody even batted an eyelash. Nobody even had eyelashes!

Hidden within their aching and amorous bodies, in the middle of all that frenzied lovemaking, something was exchanged between them. Not just emotionally, though that too seemed to reach its logical and purgative end, but physically. They could both feel it.

The seed that had been born out of the spleenfruit was passed back and forth clandestinely, through their loins. And this seed got to work, doing what seeds do best:

Pollinating. Fertilizing. Inseminating. Growing.

Isn't that all sex really is, anyway? A simple transfer of seeds.

Tabitha's stomach swelled up almost immediately. Round like a beach ball. Blue veins hugging the sides of her distended skin, bellybutton popped outward like a turkey thermometer.

She was suddenly pregnant. Very pregnant.

Despite the fact that the post-orgasmic serotonin still swirling through their brains had left them feeling like they were the only two people in the world, there was one other creature who was certainly paying attention to this carnal deed. It watched, wordless, from an aisle away.

The last time we were here, in the Home Depot, when Harrison and Tabitha first met all those years ago, we were the only ones who were watching. They had no idea. We had been there the whole time. We're here still. Observing and omnipotent, we are. The readers of this book—as far as the Mosses were concerned—just a step down from God Himself.

This time though: it is not only us who watches, but a creature far more vindictive than I would like to assume we're capable of being. As such, it is the actions of this merciless and voyeuristic creature that serve as the catalyst of rest of this tale.

Yes, we have reached the end.

The final scene.

Buckle your fucking seatbelt, people.

This is it.

The climax.

It was a worm who was watching them, standing right next to where our invisible body would be. But this was not just any worm. This was the bifurcated halves of both The Worm Woman and The Worm Man, now fused back together into a singular beast. A Frankenstein's monster of meat and slime, refabricated from the ravaged love of our two main characters.

Is this even biologically possible? Can two severed halves from two separate worms fuse together into one? Can they stalk and hunt, waiting for the perfect moment to strike, such as this worm was in the process of doing now?

Look, if these are the kind of questions you find yourself asking, and yet you've acknowledged any of the other logical incongruities and absurdities that preceded this moment, then you'll probably be displeased to know that YES, THIS TOO IS COMPLETELY IMPOSSIBLE! SCIENTIFICALLY SPEAKING, THIS IS NOT HOW WORMS WORK! AND TO EXTRAPOLATE, THIS IS NOT HOW RELATIONSHIPS ARE SUPPOSED TO WORK EITHER!

Guess what? Sometimes things don't work the way you think they should. You just have to accept it and move on.

So here's what did happen:

The worm halves met in the center of town. They rolled out of their unceremonious graves – one from a warehouse nightclub and the other from the house on Sycamore Lane – bloody and beaten and left for dead. They writhed, blindly, across this horrid landscape like fleshy steamrollers bound for a head-on collision. And once they did collide, it was a consummation not unlike that which Harrison and Tabitha just experienced, though this was much more visceral and disturbing in its display.

Their bodies tangled up like the ropes that hung in that aisle of the hardware store. Like a knot, sliding down, getting tighter and tighter. A living noose, feeding on itself. Skin melted into skin, organs ensnared with other organs, intestines like lassos pulling each other closer and closer until the delineation between "she" and "he" had lost all meaning and their focus and thoughts became that of one mind in resolution to one singular and myopic goal, as all-consuming as it was simple:

DESTROY EVERYTHING.

25

The Worm plowed towards them, charging down the aisle. Its body was chaos, barely wrangled. The creature from the darkness had no use for love. Instead it only lusted for destruction. The Worm's role was finally made clear. It was not made to be petty, like Harrison and Tabitha. It was not subject to mood swings or emotional jaunts. It was not haunted by its past, by all of history behind it, by expectation, by the divorce between idealism and reality and all the obfuscated places between, in which our human protagonists seemed to constantly wallow. It was here to do one thing and one thing only.

It was The Worm, The Eater of Worlds, The King of the Dirt, Digester of Death.

It slammed carelessly against the massive hardware racks lined up like labyrinth hedges on either side of them. They creaked as they wobbled, back and forth, before tumbling over. Like dominos, one into another. The Worm did not care about the mess it made. Merchandise spilled all over the place, clattering to the ground in a cacophonic clap. Screwdrivers rained down in the Home Depot like Holy Nails thrown from Heaven.

"Harrison?" a nervous Tabitha said. "Is that…"

"Don't think," her husband shouted, grabbing her by the hand. "Just run!"

He pulled her behind him as the two of them took off running. When the end comes, what else can you do but run?

Of course, they didn't get far. They didn't even make it out of the store. The Worm moved as fluidly as the air itself. Harrison and Tabitha's clumsy legs couldn't carry them quickly enough. This thing had gained on them, terrorized them from behind, and there was nothing they could've done to stop it.

In its wake, The Worm left destruction, impersonal and cold. It cared not for the other insects and worms in the store, some of whom were impaled by the falling shrapnel or crushed beneath tilting scaffolds. It cared not for itself or its own wellbeing. Cuts and abrasions ran up and down its frame, its putrid blood splashed against the concrete. This worm was a missile, homed in on its target: the reunited Mosses desperately trying to escape it.

The Worm whipped itself forward, lunging like a boomerang, and wrapped the top half of its torso around Tabitha's ankles.

She tripped. Fell face first. The impact on her stomach mound sent her immediately into contractions. She was in labor. Amniotic fluid shot down her thighs, warm and pink. Whatever had rapidly grown inside her womb was ready to come out. And The Worm couldn't allow that. It wouldn't allow that. It was its job to make sure the new day never sees its dawn. It had been tasked by the universe – by the very laws of Nature Itself – to tear this couple apart. Emotionally. Then physically, if the need be.

The Worm wrapped up around her, a tornado of balmy flesh that whisked her away from her screaming husband, Harrison screaming "Noooooooooooooo!" as it pulled her the rest of the way through the store and then out the front entrance, back into the streets.

It took off, towards downtown.

26

Harrison burst through the front doors of the Home Depot, spinning his head from left to right, searching for any sign as to where Tabitha and her captor had gone. His skin felt hot and tight, like it wasn't skin at all, but rather a wetsuit he had been forced to squeeze into. His heart *ka-thudded* in his chest, pumping spleenfruit sap through his veins.

He heard his wife scream, in the distance, an exasperated yip echoing across the cave, the acoustics making it seem like it was coming at him from all directions at once. Then there was a crash, then more commotion. He strained his leaf-filled ears, until he was able to pinpoint its source. It was coming from the right. He looked. From here he could see the city skyline, and beyond that, the volcano sticking up taller than the buildings like a giant, ashy finger.

"I'm coming," he said to his wife, though she couldn't hear him. "I'm coming to rescue you."

The Worm held Tabitha so tight she could barely breathe. This was, of course, no concern for The Worm. The creature had no concerns at all beyond the most pressing and obvious one, which was to take Tabitha up to the top of the volcano and toss her inside, into the magma.

"You want to do what?!" Tabitha gasped as she read that last paragraph and the monster's true intent was finally revealed to her.

"You're going to kill me?"

Yes. Yes, indeed it was.

"But why?"

Oh Tabitha. Silly Tabitha. Naïve Tabitha. Soon-to-be-dead Tabitha. This is the way this story ends. C'mon now, you had to expect something like this, no? Why would I put a volcano in this book if I didn't intend to throw someone into it? I've alluded to it before: you know as well as I do that there's no poetry in a story that ends with *happily-ever-after.* That is not how good literature works! You have to die. If anyone reading this is going to feel vindicated, you have to die. I have to sacrifice you. For them.

"What are you talking about?! I don't give a fuck about the people reading this!" she cried out. "I care about ME! I care about my husband! And my life! And you should care about me, too. You all should. Can't you see that I'M the main character!?"

No, Tabitha. WE'RE the main characters. All of us: The worms. The readers. The person writing this sentence, right now. This is a story about us, not you. You and Harrison are just the tools I've employed in this allegory; you are the proxies onto which we can ascribe our own thoughts and feelings. You're not real. None of this is real. You look different in the mind of every person who imagines you. The city is built differently in every single person's head. Your body, your relationship, the entire fucking universe you inhabit: it's all just a fabrication. You are in no more real peril than the person reading this book is in real peril. You can't actually die, because you never existed in the first place.

"It's not true." A tear rolled down her cheek. "The things I'm feeling are real, whether I'm just a character in a story or not. I deserve better than this terrible ending. We all deserve better than this."

The Worm made it up to the top of the volcano and held her out over the mouth of the open pit. The ground rumbled and orange waves slopped and popped in the bubbling inferno below.

Tabitha closed her eyes and said goodbye.

"Goodbye."

But then:

"Stop!" a voice suddenly interrupted.

The Worm slowly turned.

There stood Harrison, right behind them. His body was overrun with gashes, thousands of micro-slits, out of which plant matter spilled, along with fingers. Weird, knotty fingers. Fingers attached to the branches sticking awkwardly out of his skin. His feet dug into the ground, anchor themselves in the dirt. The hand that used to be a hand, and then was a shovel, was now a series of dangling vines longer than he was tall. He raised one of those vines and pointed it threateningly at The Worm.

"Let her go," Harrison said, his normally ineffectual tone now replaced by a voice much deeper, much more confident. Perhaps this was the first sentence he had ever spoken that he actually believed in. It certainly sounded that way.

The Worm shook its head and looked at this shrub of a man with the kind of pity you'd normally reserve for a sick animal. It was barely pity at all. There was something much more insidious woven into its movements. No, this wasn't pity.

It was more like...mockery.

And The Worm let go of Tabitha and she fell into the lava.

As seed-addled as Harrison's brain may have been, his synapses were still firing on all of their cylinders – like a ray gun going *pew pew pew* – and time seemed to slow down.

This was not a moment that required any more contemplation. No more long-winded diatribes on the fleeting nature of love. It was too much contemplation that got us into this mess in the first place, second guessing ourselves out of happiness, not knowing how fragile such a concept was. Stop thinking so hard, Harrison Moss. We don't need any more inner monologues. We need ACTION.

The Worm smugly stood there, knowing it had won. That it would always win. That this was the natural order of things. And that people like Harrison, and people like us, like you and I, would come and go, would endlessly pass by, the death river flowing like an unending sieve, as the bottom of the food chain rises to the top, and the worms process both the princes and the paupers, the lovers and losers alike.

And Harrison dove into the volcano after his wife.

And then they both died.

The end.

27

Okay, okay, okay. They didn't die. Not at that exact moment, at least. One day, in the future, they will certainly perish, as do we all. But as for right now, what actually happened was this:

The ground shook. MAN OH MAN did the ground shake! It was an earthquake that seemed to come out of nowhere, but it was Richter-tipping to a magnitude by which mankind had never seen. They'd have to invent a new unit of measurement just to classify an earthquake as severe as this. THAT'S how strong it was!

And why did this earthquake happen, right then? It certainly wasn't fate or divine intervention, I'll tell you that much. It was more like…luck. Because sometimes the earth shakes and you can't predict where or when and for how long or how hard. That's just how it is. So this moment was merely fortuitous. Perhaps it was too fortuitous to be believed. THIS IS BULLSHIT, you say. There just happened to be an earthquake RIGHT NOW, at the most climatic part?

Yeah, motherfucker. There was. The signs were there all along, foreshadowed throughout this whole book. If you knew where to look, you would've seen them. It's not my fault you can't understand subtext.

So the ground shook and the magma in the bowl of this volcano shook with it. And all that shaking caused the magma to do some peculiar things, like releasing great big columns of pillaring steam. And before Harrison could even cross the threshold of this volcano's brim, one of those geysers of steam knocked him backwards onto his ass, back on the ground. The impact caused leaves to shoot out of his nose and mouth and ears in such profusion he disappeared beneath the bush.

And the ground shook harder.

Pieces of the ceiling broke loose and fell, mighty stalactites millions of years old crashed down to the surface below. The buildings surrounding the base of the mountain collapsed. They fell over as easily as dominos pushed by a lazy child. Insects were crushed beneath the debris, worms tried to burrow and escape, but the rumbling ground exhumed them back up to the top, only to be splattered alongside the rest of the vermin. There was no escaping this.

Soon, downtown was nothing more than a pile of rubble. And then the ground split open, wide like a canyon, and the soil beneath it gave way.

A gaping hole opened up.

Another hole!

But this one was deeper and blacker than the one Harrison and Tabitha had tumbled down the first time. The suburbs and the city, the ocean of blood that surrounded it and the monstrous creatures that swam in its depths – ALL OF IT – slid down into the chasm, into a newer, deeper level of Earth completely obscured from our humble view. Everything fell away, piece by piece, except for the erupting volcano, The Worm, and the man who was standing on the edge of its rim. Not even Tabitha could be counted among those still trapped in this collapsing cave, because as the volcano hissed and spat, a big fiery bubble formed on the boiling meniscus, growing bigger than a fiery bubble ought to grow, and then it popped, releasing a massive blast of rising steam.

And sitting atop that column of invisible steam was Tabitha. Her tiny body shooting upwards. A reverse meteorite heading towards the surface, from the inside of the Earth.

She rose quickly, too quickly to be seen, smashing through the upper crust that sealed off this domed city beneath the dirt. Harrison blinked and she was gone.

She passed through the layers of sediment as if they were as soft as marshmallow. The centrifugal force by which she was thrust left her burning hot and gasping for air, but when she burst through the ground, back to the surface of the world she had come from, shooting upward ever still, the westward breeze now cooling her blistered skin to the point that frost formed on the tips of her toes. And she went higher, a contrail of smoke trailing behind her. She looked down and could see Sycamore Lane, the REAL Sycamore Lane that she had lived on with Harrison for so many years: her home, her neighborhood around it, her entire life laid out below her like the last crumbs at a lunch buffet. She reached out for it, but she was rising too fast. In an instant, it was reduced to nothing more than a speck beneath her. Then the city was reduced to speck-status behind it, disappearing into a tiny point on the azimuth.

The atmosphere that surrounded the globe was shaped like a cavern itself, but bigger. It protected the Earth from the harshness of space, sealing us off from the rest of the cosmos. In all these years under the sky, how had she not realized it? They had always been trapped in a cave, of sorts. The world presented itself to her in concentric circles, infinitely above as it was below. The size of her cage merely one based on perspective. And right then her perspective was HUGE, and getting wider the further away she traveled. Is there beauty in that? Maybe. But it was a question whose nuances Tabitha would have to ponder later, because as the air became thin and cold and she gasped for breath, and the blackness of outer space now reached down into the ionosphere to pull her forward with the same tenacity in which the fire below pushed her up, something else was happening to her body. And much like the earthquake that had just trembled beneath their feet, this event too can come at a moment suspiciously convenient, if not wholly unplanned:

She was about to give birth.

Meanwhile, still trapped under the ground, Harrison stood and watched helplessly as his wife once again disappeared beyond his grasp.

He wanted to leap into the volcano again, to ride a different shaft of heat like a leaf upon a zephyr, to the furthest annals of space and beyond that if he had to, if that's where his wife had gone. He thought it would be romantic. The ultimate sacrifice. But he knew that at this point, even if his plan worked and he wasn't incinerated instantly in the viscous lava below, he would still be behind her, chasing her, forever trying to catch up.

That would not do. Not anymore. He realized then, if he truly wanted to be with her, that it was time to step completely out of the routines and patterns they had dug for themselves. There was no longer any turning back. It was time to try something completely different. Completely new. It was time to end this book in a way that would've been impossible to predict, even with all the painfully obvious metaphors I had left you with along with way. It was time to grow. Or die.

And so, instead of actively fighting the seed that had been sprouting inside him – the seed he voluntarily swallowed for reasons that, until now, had not been totally clear to him – he decided to embrace it. He pushed. He flexed every fiber in his being. Flexed so hard his skin completely split apart, shedding off him in sheets, tearing like wet paper towel, and a newer version of himself expanded outward from the cocoon.

He grew big. He grew fast. He was a spleenfruit tree, and he sprouted thousands of times faster than bamboo. His bark pulled taut against the dowels of his bones. His veins flowed with sanguine sap. His feet burrowed into the side of the volcano and down into its flaming basin, the lava not hot enough to penetrate his new husky shell, the magma nothing more than a puddle for a creature his size. His toes twisted their way down, filling up every inch of every channel with his expanding body, until they were hooked around the iron core at the center of the Earth itself.

The Worm, who had once seemed so sinister and so in control, had been rendered almost microscopic in comparison to Harrison now. The threat it had presented was all but forgot. We will not even mention it again.

Fingers covered his massive arms. Twisted fingers, some twenty knuckles long. They were everywhere, millions of them, digging through the soil as Harrison forced them up through the ceiling of the cave, into the dirt above.

From the ends of these fingers dangled fruit, purple and meaty, the shape and color of a human spleen.

He continued to grow. Doubling each passing second. And soon, he filled the entire cavern, his back and shoulders pressing against the sides. There was nowhere left for him to go but out.

* * *

Tabitha rocketed through outer space. Mars just passed her on the left. Then there went Jupiter, on her right. She opened up her legs, spread them wide, straining harder than she had ever strained before. She pushed. Pushed. PUSHED!

And out it came.

Her baby was born. Except it wasn't a baby at all.

The thing that slithered its way out of her womb was the only thing her and her husband's turbulent communion could have possibly created:

She gave birth to a supermassive black hole.

Tabitha passed out from the exertion. Giving birth to a supermassive black hole was a grueling and uncomfortable process. What's more, because there was no oxygen in space, and it's subfreezing all the time, once Tabitha passed out, she was not going to wake up again. And because space was a vacuum and created no friction, she was still hurtling away from her former planet at the same speed in which the volcano had shot her. It's pretty crazy, when you think about it: how we're all hurtling through space. The Earth and the Sun and the Solar System and the entire galaxy as a whole. All moving so damn fast, all the time.

Harrison's spleenfruit tree arms grew in opposite directions. One to the left and one to the right, like magnets repelled from each other. They worked their way through the dirt until they came out of the ground at polar ends of the Earth; antipodes stretched across the x-axis of his torso. The arms rose up, much like the spleenfruit tree in the Moss' backyard had. And if these trees happened to sprout out of the yard of some other discontented couple, perhaps the forbidden fruit it bore would be as tempting as it had been to Harrison and Tabitha. Perhaps the worm, like the Biblical Snake, will whisper sweet lies in their weary heads. Perhaps they will pluck the fruit and they will eat it and this whole fucked up story can go on repeating itself, again and again, for as long as the words 'I love you' are able to gild themselves upon human lips.

Regardless, these arms reached up taller and thicker than any other trees before them. They cast shadows across neighborhoods that had never known shadows before. They wrapped themselves around the planet, like they were giving it a giant hug, and they braced themselves in the deepest parts of the ocean. The displaced water sent tidal waves crashing into coastal cities, washing away hundreds of thousands of lives, but this was of no concern to Harrison. The forces of nature were beyond his control.

Veins on the surface of his bark-like skin throbbed as he dug his fingers into the Earth and pulled upward. He lifted his body up into the dirt. Just like a worm himself, he was forced to swallow and shit out the soil in front of him, there was nowhere else for it to go but through him and out the other end.

Miles, he had to pull himself. Up towards the surface. That earthquake was but a preamble to the rumble the world experienced now. Miles he pulled, and cities he shook, and then he finally breached. His nose first, larger than a mountain now, followed soon by his lips, parting like the Grand Canyon, and his eyeballs bigger than two twin moons. He blinked and it sounded like thunder. He took a breath and the whole world trembled.

But Harrison had no time to enjoy the amenities the topside offered him—the fresh oxygen and a yellow sun—because his bride was flying across the vast reaches of space like a lost little comet without an orbit to call its own.

And even more: the supermassive black hole she had given birth to had set up shop not too far away and had begun the process of consuming everything in its vicinity, much in the way the hungriest worm would only ever aspire to—tearing space itself apart on the molecular level, rearranging those bits in the mysterious and unsympathetic way that a black hole does, destroying the stars and the moons and the billions upon billions of worlds splayed out across them like lonely nodes in a cosmic game of connect-the-dots.

This black hole was darker and deeper than anything Harrison could've ever created alone. Darker and deeper than he could even fathom. It cared not for them, or for anyone or anything. THIS was the hole, the final hole he had dug, the one from which there truly was no escape, the result of their tumultuous love, containing every sadness and every joy, now bigger and stronger than everything it touched. Unstoppable.

* * *

The Earth shook apart, fell out of orbit, got sucked towards the vortex at the center of this insatiable dark thing. Harrison flapped his giant spleenfruit tree arms, trying to paddle his planet away from its inevitable destruction. But it was no use. He couldn't fight it. And out there, somewhere beyond sight, Tabitha floated, bloated and blue and covered in ice.

His body was still growing. How big was he going to get, he wondered? Under the crust of the hollow Earth his body, a countless mass of dirty roots and whispering tendrils, had filled up every inch.

And Tabitha, bluer and colder still.

"Goddamn it!" Harrison screamed. And his voice was so loud it could be heard by everyone, everywhere, at the same time. Even beyond the fictional universe in which he existed, his voice carried beyond this storybook's lowly pages and floated through your head, just now. You heard them, didn't you? You have to concentrate. *Really* listen. This is happening all around you, happening to you. Just listen as he repeats himself:

"GODDAMN IT!" he's crying out.

You heard it that time, no?

Well, even if you can't hear him, you can certainly feel him: he's digging the tips of his spleenfruit fingers into the ground, deeper. He is grabbing the ground with no more resistance than if he were to grab a loaf of bread. And he's screaming again. YES, I KNOW YOU CAN HEAR IT THIS TIME because it's not an actual scream, but a figurative one. His scream represents the feeling of every insecurity, every doubt you've ever had. It's not an actual noise. It's a whisper from the darkest part of your soul. You are full of his screams. You are made up of more of his screams than you are of yourself.

He screamed and pulled.

The terrain under our feet broke apart. Dirt danced and shimmied, but no worms surfaced from this restless landscape. There were no worms anymore. There was only us. We were the worms.

The ground split open. It split open down the middle, the crack running like the equator, all the way around. Harrison's two giant hands extended from the center of the Earth, pulled and ripped the entire planet completely in half. The shell of the Earth came apart like it was merely glass. Chunks of land broke away and were thrown out into space. Entire continents were cast off the planet in an instant. AND THEN: the supermassive black hole swallowed up all the remains. The leftover pieces of this eggshell Earth, sucked inside its insatiable dark belly. The nothingness inside the black hole, eternal and inevitable, growing stronger and more ferocious with every atom it consumed.

But Harrison was free of the life underground that had imprisoned him for so long. Free of the surface even, that imprisoned him too, but in a different way. With no more land to call his home, he was his own planet now, about the size and shape of the one he had just sacrificed.

Planet Harrison clawed his way across empty space, dragging his damaged, muddy body through the lightyears that separated Tabitha from him. Pain no longer mattered. It was there, of course, but he ignored it. He would endure this pain forever, if need be. Until:

There she was. Tabitha. He had caught up to her. Her body encased in ice. Floating in front of him again, finally within his massive grasp.

He reached out and wrapped his giant spleenfruit hands around her frozen frame. He pulled her close to him. She was almost invisible in comparison to his current stature, but as the only other being on Planet Harrison's body, he knew she was there, even if he couldn't see her.

He held her tight. Up against his body. She lay on his surface, like a glacier.

Heat radiated out from his core, a kind of biological forge that was somehow able to sustain him once his body reached planetary status. If we could all be as big as planets, perhaps we could generate our own heat too.

The fire in him was faint, but he focused all his energy into it and pressed Tabitha's tiny carcass up against it. And slowly, she thawed. The ice around her melted in thick droplets, filling the empty riverbeds and tributaries that covered his skin, and her blood flowed again the way it supposed to, and her lungs pumped air, and her eyes opened glassy and wide, and she looked up at her celestial-sized husband with the same kind of tenderness she looked at the sunrise the morning after they had gotten married.

"Harrison?" she said.

"Yes Tabitha," he sighed with relief, lakes of tears rolling out of his asteroid eyes. "Yes, it's me."

"You're—you're a planet now?" she said, slightly confused.

"I destroyed the Earth," he said. "I had to, to save you."

She sat up and looked backwards, across all that empty space, to where the Earth used to float. In its place, the supermassive black hole swirled, distorting space-time all around it, sucking everything into its maw. Destroying it forever.

"Is that our baby?" she asked.

"Yes," he said. "You are a mother. Congratulations."

Tabitha frowned.

"This is the ending?"

He nodded, yes.

"It seems bittersweet," she said.

"Of course it is," he said. "If entropy is the state into which all things are eventually drawn, to allow love to flourish, to allow us to exist, we must be ready to fight the natural order."

"It's too much," she sniffled, beginning to sob. "It's too much to ask of people. We're expected to tear the universe apart in our wake? And for what? To have a slim chance at happiness?"

Planet Harrison sighed and said, "Yes."

And so it came to pass: a slim chance at happiness they were afforded.

Tabitha built a house on her husband's surface. It looked just like the house they left behind on Sycamore Lane. She tilled Harrison's soil, just like a worm, and in return, he grew for her the spleenfruit which sustained her. They still fought on occasion. They had good days and bad days, boring days and exciting ones. That's how it works.

In the distance, the supermassive black hole still loomed. There was no getting rid of it. There were only moments like this, where two lovers allowed themselves to be together, just beyond its horizon. Perhaps on this new world they will finally figure out who they really are, deep down inside. Find out what they truly have to offer, to themselves, and each other.

It won't be easy. It never is.

And so, as we close out this novel, I am going leave you with this simple epilogue, not a moral exactly, but hopefully satisfying in some way, nonetheless:

Harrison and Tabitha Moss didn't necessarily live happily-ever-after.

But—goddamn it—together, they lived.

DANGER SLATER is the world's most flammable writer. He is the author of *Love Me*, *DangerRama*, *I Will Rot Without You* and *Puppet Skin*. Originally from New Jerssey, he now resides in Portland, OR.

Visit him online at dangerslater.blogspot.com

CPSIA information can be obtained
at www.ICGtesting.com
Printed in the USA
LVHW11s2309101018
593211LV00001B/36/P

9 781621 052562